Crucible of Pain

Jesse Stanton

Crucible of Pain

Vanguard Press

VANGUARD PAPERBACK

A CIP catalogue record for this title is
available from the British Library.

ISBN 978 1 80016 961 6

*Vanguard Press is an imprint of
Pegasus Elliot Mackenzie Publishers Ltd.*
www.pegasuspublishers.com

First Published in 2024

**Vanguard Press
Sheraton House Castle Park
Cambridge England**

Printed & Bound in Great Britain

To my family and friends: thank you for all of the love and support. I hope you enjoy my story.

My leg was gripped and shaken violently as I snapped into consciousness, taken from the dreary dreamscape that I had learned to appreciate over the years. I opened both weary eyes as I pulled my numb arm out from under my pillow and looked toward my leg, finding it clutched by beautifully pellucid, ghostly hands. Still being shook, I flipped over to have my back against the bed.

Fuck. Time to move, I thought, as I twisted my head upwards. I knew what was to come next. The flat, staticky shimmer formed across the top of my domed housing, beginning at my switched off ceiling light, spreading eerily towards the edges of the room, and filling it like a gentle smoke with minute snaps of electricity popping intermittently. It came steadily down and aligned itself horizontally with my body. The Veil was falling. I gritted my teeth and clenched my jaw to flex particular muscles in my ears, working against The Veil's preferred method of entering my mind. I felt a twitch of the lobes. The touch of The Veil spread across my forehead and crawled, wriggling from there into my ear canals. I fought against its movement, straining my jaw as hard as I could without breaking my teeth. Still, it gently crept in.

Muscle spasms and itches in my face and body confirmed that The Veil activation still brought those damn e-slugs in. They came from beyond the digital reactor pinned to the space above my room and dropped like tears from the ceiling. I pinched at the electronic bugs that landed on and near my body and threw them off one by one, tossing them to the far spaces of the rounded room before they latched on and seeped static slime onto my body. The critters left a burning, phantom itch for hours if I didn't pick them off fast enough.

I struggled against The Veil as I picked off e-slugs and kicked away the hands at my legs. The Veil never lost this little game of tug of war we played, but it did not stop me from putting up a fight. Its light hold on my mind seemed a bit heavier lately.

Slightly upset at the loss, yet satisfied with the effort put forth, I unclenched my jaw and turned my attention to the hands that protruded from the electronic formation. "*God damn it Ghostie, stop, I'm up,*" I communicated mentally. I took a moment waiting to 'hear' Ghostie's responses, waiting for her subvocalization to crescendo into the softest of audible whispers in my head. I used this time to clench life back into my fist, opening and closing my fingers as though donating blood. Going from numb, unresponsive hands to nerves firing pins and needles through my fingertips was a pleasurable pain that I had grown accustomed to. This was the result of putting my arm under my pillow and head until it went numb. Locking my arms like that at night to achieve sleep had been working thus far, though I was unsure of whether I had been passing out or falling asleep. A technique I liked to refer to as a sleeper hold. It was the only sound way for me to rest any more.

Now that The Veil was fully embraced, my thoughts became shared thoughts. 'Shared' meaning I could connect and communicate with Ghostic and the people of The Company, more specifically the requests department, through the power of The Veil, and they now could form thoughts discernable from mine. Ghostie, my partner, was stuck with me, stuck within The Veil, stuck in a memory of what she once was. Her form was humanlike, lacking in specific features apart from her eyes and hands. She was incomplete, a changing pattern of hard light and digital mist, in a constant state of holding herself together while falling apart. She was able to interact with the physical world if she chose, by drawing the hard light to her hands. I remained unsure, but hopeful that Ghostie's words were in fact her own, as I knew the Veil pulled from language I understood, translated her energy , and placed it to a fitting vocabulary, which was then vocalized in my mind. It was a fuzzy connection. Some days it felt like I was talking to myself. To my knowledge she was one of the first movers here. Perished during her work at The Company. I mentally told the e-slugs to shove off , and they crawled up to the ceiling, back to the reactor.

Ghostie's whispers in my mind grew. I focused to hear them. What I believed to be a playful overabundance of cursing and name-calling had become commonplace between us and had served as a type of sound check to make sure that at least most words were perceivable.

"*What*?" I thought with exclamation.

"All I caught was shithead, worthless, and something about wasted space."

"You fucker, it's time for work," she responded, her words audible only in my head. I got out of bed as The Veil conformed snuggly to my body like an itchy glove to a hand.

"How you doin' Ghostie? Gonna let me see that beautiful face of yours today?" I asked mentally. Days and nights were merely rough estimates, broken apart by work, downtime, and sleep. I was without a clock for time, in a room without windows. Ghostie would not let me see her face fully since we started the job because she put out veiled waste in the manner of blinding light from her eyes. She was becoming fairly proficient at adjusting the intensity. Every now and then I could catch a glimpse of her hovering around my peripherals. She responded with a litany of vulgarities once again.

That's my girl, I thought as I flicked on the light. The dim base lighting in the domed room turned to a bright sunny daylike quality. I took my pajamas off and got dressed. Underwear, jeans, a T-shirt, a hooded sweatshirt, some socks, and sneakers, keeping things simple. No showers or washing of clothes were necessary with The Veil's cleansing touch in the morning, and no food was necessary to provide energy in its presence. I did not eat, and I did not bathe. Couldn't keep much food down anyways, my mouth had become just a place with which to expel excessiveness. All sexual urges had been torn from me, hindered along with hair growth. I remained

10

unsure if I had been aging properly. There were no doors in my workroom. I was told, "Save for great emergency, when the work is done the door will be installed." The adventure I chose. A two-foot by two-foot, metal vent opened in the wall, alongside another vent leading into a garbage chute. The first vent is where I found my favorite brand of stimulant concoction. I took the drink and downed it before passing an envelope of fingernail clippings from the day before into the opening. I had to trade a small piece of myself daily to be used in Veil synchronization.

A piece of myself to become more than myself, I thought as I passed the clippings through and mentally prepared for the day ahead.

The work routine started with The Veil's load in of The Companies handpicked, previously performed movements that had taken place days before, and it began guiding my body. I had found many of these procedures through freestyle movement built upon the rigid routine that these jobs always began with. The Veil guided me, harnessing my brainpower to set myself into an exact position of where those moves began and ended, stimulating muscles to ensure the move's completion. It felt as though someone touched me beneath my skin, and pushed me towards deviations from those original movements. I was glad to hear The Veil had been upgraded with a masking ability during this job that allowed my face to be free from that part of the process. The surprising contortion of muscles in the face under abnormal circumstances was invasive and uncomfortable. I had also found it difficult to perform the physical work with my face being twisted and tugged about. The work routine continued until the unique movement requirements had been met and The Veil along with my handler Ghostie were satisfied. This could last several hours or as little as one hour. Through communication with Ghostie, who had taken a leading role on the job, and trial and error we had cut the process down, doing as little as possible to save my energy for freestyle movement and flow of thought for later in the day.

Starting off with the easy ones, I turned the small heater in my room on low, sat down on my bed and began to crack my knuckles. Simple and satisfying. I could do this indefinitely, which is convenient because I had to do some movements five or six times before The Veil registered it as a new move. It would notify me through a small electric shiver throughout my body, the more in depth, lengthy, and difficult the movement, the more intense the shiver. I cracked my knuckles repeatedly, moving my hands in distinct positions trying to find ways different from days before. I took my time like trying to crack a safe, holding my right hand up to my left ear to listen to the bubbles in my joints collapse into an enjoyable crunch, and after about a minute of this, I felt a small, yet gratifying electric shiver rise from the base of my spine to the top of my skull. I continued doing the easier moves until The Veil loaded in something more difficult and I cranked the heater up a click.

Now standing I could feel the thin layer of The Veil guiding me into varying positions, being pushed into deviations of those positions, and then deviations of those deviations. With the heater on and Ghostie's coaching, I started chasing down warmth, my muscles loosened up, and I fell into a good rhythm. I moved as fluidly as possible from position to position, racking up electric shivers consistently. After an hour or so, Ghostie and The Veil seemed satiated with movement, and I sat down on my bed, readying myself for the emotional crucible.

The Veil began gently probing me for emotional stimulation, which I always thought was strange because it's not something I could feel physically. I thought of the crucible processes as a type of distillery, the crucible perfected the deepest feelings of human emotion of varying grades, over many years. It all began simply enough but had grown to be something complex and overpowering at times. Those feelings would be harvested by The Veil and sold by The Company as an electronic experience to those brave enough to 'try them on', and recycled at The Company itself to be built upon. Whenever I felt unsure about this process, I was encouraged by Ghostie that the harvested emotional samples had a 'multitude of uses'. The Veil tended to focus on one a day. Feeling uneasy having endured intense moments of emotional exploration while in the crucible state, I remained distrustful of this part of the process. I prepared myself mentally. I could feel it starting, and instinctively braced against it, not knowing what to expect. A heat began in my stomach, rising to my chest and head. Something positive? An overpowering pressure in my chest and head formed. With my body feeling like I was standing out in the sun, all the warmth and comfort of the world within me, tears begin falling uncontrollably at the beauty of what had taken over so unexpectedly, which alleviated some of the lingering pressure from my head and chest. I searched for words to put to the emotion that could describe it. After several minutes of this it slowly dissipated. Were those tears of joy, of love? Strange without a subject to place it to. I checked my peripherals to ensure Ghostie was with me as the feelings began to fade, leaving a stagnant chill inside me. I turned the heater up a click.

Cooling down as the heater warmed up, I had a chat with Ghostie. It was time to freestyle, create something to build on for the following days, physically and mentally.

"What are we doing today, Ghostie?" I asked mentally.

"I wanna see some kung fu," she communicated softly. Surprised at the request, I audibly laughed.

Not while I'm sober! I thought with excitement. After the rigidity of the work routine, it was commonplace for me to have many drinks, relaxing the muscles in my body, providing more fluidity to movements, expelling self-doubt, and making movement cast in The Veil more enjoyable overall. I mentally requested to have some silver tequila delivered to the room. I did not eat, I did not bathe, and due to restorative properties of The Veil, I did not suffer from hangovers. After a few minutes, the vent popped open with a fifth of the clear liquid. A couple swigs later, I was feeling warm again. Not knowing any forms or disciplines of martial arts I shot up from the bed with enthusiasm and took several stances, then began to hone wild punches and kicks against my imaginary opponent. This continued for an hour or so, evolving into critically injuring those imaginary opponents with periodic sips of alcohol after an electric shiver was felt.

"See Ghostie, that's how you break the enemy's knee, from the side of the leg which they have all the weight on," I communicated mentally.

"Good shit,," she responded, seeing her shapes within my peripherals I tried to focus on her while looking at something else, and made a good effort to slap her translucent hand for a high five, expecting a satisfying pop, but she shifted her physical form to let it pass through her freely. She laughed inside of my head, and I snickered aloud and turned the heater up a click.

"What's next, ghost?" I asked mentally, sitting down to catch a bit of breath.

"Call-outs,," she responded. I jumped up, feeling a bit bouncy with the right amount of alcohol in me. She proceeded to tell a list of actions, that I was to do my best to create in a single room without props, ranging from becoming monsters and creating their gait patterns, to dancing in as many styles as I could muster, all movement recorded in the shroud of The Veil, and applied within The Company. I mentally requested some musical accompaniment, to find rhythm, and got to work. My imagination fired up to create horrible abominations of terror, twisted flesh and teeth, and then I tried to become them. I would walk for hours with my body contorted in strange ways in accordance with the image of what I was trying to replicate in my head. Each time something new, with The Veil moving me to become an effigy of what we were trying to create, molding me to it, alongside Ghostie calling out to be 'faster', or 'move your arms more' and other nitpicks to create a product to build from. The nature of the movement was not as important as the movement itself. These wild or rigid motions would serve as something to be built on in later days. I would feel foolish for doing all these strange things if not for Ghostie's seriousness to feed off, as well as copious amounts of alcohol. Feeling a grandiose heat building in the room, I turned the heater down a click.

Sitting down again to catch my breath, I thought, *Next up, Ghostie?*

"Exercises in poetic thought,," she replied.

"Okay, give me a minute," I communicated, requesting the music to shut off, and taking another sip of tequila while calming down and preparing the framework in my mind.

"Wringing the body of water
An ocean before
The ocean before me
All in the mind,
All in the world

Electricity…"

I paused.

"More," Ghostie whispered.

Hold on, I thought.

"We got a schedule to keep so hurry it up,," she replied in a rushed tone. I mentally requested a flip open lighter. Moments later, the vent opened, and I had the metal lighter in my hands along with a memo with familiar words on it: fire hazard, you've been warned. I began to flick it open, light it and shut in as many unconventional ways as I could. Something to occupy me while I thought, searching my mind for format.

"Thought torn from the pages of mind
Communication I find
Wondering what yours is and what is mine
A gift given, gift taken, all is fine
Seeds watered
Seeds heated
Breaking of shells
Mind tapped
Puzzle wrapped
My self to sell
Harmony…
…At least parts of me."

I paused to stretch my mind for more vocabulary.

"More," Ghostie conveyed quickly. I continued.

"Movement, fluidity
Thoughtless stupidity
Thought less rigidity

Talk less, you and me
Think more placidity
Lost heat, humidity
Stimulant's acidity
Veil falls, rapidity
Veil rises, aridity…"
I paused again.

"Opposites," Ghostie imparted as I took a big swig of tequila, then continued flipping the lighter about.

"Words are free to any man, chained together in the mind. Shown with the body, watch the face the mouth, emotion, unseen if unspoken, spoken with all, or spoken with silence."

"More," Ghostie communicated.

"Finding splendor in the modesty, at home with my work, destroying myself as an individual to create something similar as so many do, do not be different enough to be considered some of the same. I tear down what I have built, subtracting from the additions made to feel a cold shiver in the heat of movement, stale as my body may grow, I will die active, and give part of myself to take all that you are, not for granted, taking action undecided on the choice of taking action."

"More, slow it down," Ghostie conveyed.

"Feelings numb. Icing vocal cords while warming up thoughts in a silence, normalcy in the loud, anomalous caricatures, my own drowning in the lushness of alcohol, saved in the dry heat of electricity, using all my strength in the waking morning working towards weakness in the sleeping night. Becoming what I stray from, in order to be chaotically acceptable is exceptional."

"Good enough for one day," Ghostie communicated gently.

Awesome, I thought, returning the lighter to the open vent.

"Can we communicate vocally?" I asked mentally. My own vocal communication was acceptable during our process, though it seemed out of place at this point. I sipped on more tequila, trying to relax, yet still feeling askew from the emotional crucible earlier.

"You may, though as you know I can't do that," she said.

"Why not?" I poked.

"I don't exactly have the right equipment for that, dumbass," she responded.

"Can I see today's ranks?" I asked, testing my voice.

"Ask The Company," she replied. I mentally requested to see a chart of today's ranks, sorted according to this job, and though they wouldn't share any specific data, the numerous collections of electronic shivers were inserted into my mind, and I had my answer.

Pretty good, I thought as I began fidgeting my arms and hands.

"I thought we weren't tracking records this time," Ghostie conveyed.

"True, just curious," I said.

The constant tracking of numbers and rankings had lost much time as well as appeal while honing the moves on previous jobs. I thought of the past jobs and adventures I had been on, Ghostie being there solely for this job which has taken up half of my 'long' career. Long in terms of being there when The Company was first formed, and somehow staying with them up to this point. The adventure was what must have been several years long. Solitary horror creation was the word being tossed around when the escapade was first written. I heard rumors about it and had to be at least a part of it, whether it be requests department or one of the movers. I thought I lucked out to be picked as a mover. I would not have met Ghostie if I hadn't.

"How much longer do you think we have in here, ghost?" I asked.

"Not long if I had to guess, maybe another year. You should have requested a calendar when we began, dumbass," Ghostie whispered.

"Yeah. Hindsight," I replied.

"Anyways, what should we do now? Wanna meet a monster?" I asked.

"Yes!" Ghostie responded enthusiastically.

"I'll request one." I mentally asked for the character completion queue, and the number two came to mind. I requested a physical construct to be built of one of them, figuring I could save the other one for later in case we got lonely. The Veil stayed in my mind but the second skin that wrapped snuggly around my body began to tear away, as if the feeling of touch moved beyond the barrier of my skin and into the air around it and began to form in front of me, the gargantuan figure, starting as a large human shaped form of The Veil's energy, becoming closer to the monster that The Veil and I envisioned days prior. A truly horrific sight of large, deformed features. With teeth as big as fingers, painful to look at as they dug into the pale, mottled skin around his face. Small eyes dark as coal. Long, sinewy arms healed over from injuries of the past and blood, both wet and dry stained through what was left of its tattered clothing. The monster brought me visions of human testing and experiments gone off the rails.

"Pretty creepy," I said with a smile, wishing I could see him in action in a film or electronic experience. "I'm not good with names but he looks like a Chester," I said.

"That's a pretty shit name for a monster," Ghostie said.

"So is Ghostie," I said sarcastically. Ghostie then proceeded to curse at me in alphabetical order and explain that she was in fact not a monster. I ignored her, thinking about what level of negative emotional energy The Company would bind Chester with. Feeling a bit like Dr. Frankenstein and all the guilt that came with that was normal for me at this stage, but would Chester be better off with no emotional elements at all? Not my place to decide as a mover.

"Chester," I said extending my arm, him reciprocating, and retracting the heavy, gnarled fingernails back as his large, deformed hand embraced mine. I remained unsure if The Veil had created a physical form for him, or perhaps pulled memories of my past handshakes, points in my mind to create his physical properties, how his hand would feel to my sense of touch.

"Happy birthday," I said quietly as Chester's mangled form dissipated back into Veil energy and crept to the top of the room, resetting my sense of touch before being drawn back into my ceiling light. Glad to have met him before emotional imbuement, I turn the heater off completely.

Thinking of tomorrow, I requested a randomizer of instrumental beats of varying genres to listen to, The Company would not allow any lyrics to be heard while working, something about too much feedback. I also asked for a pair of scissors, and an envelope. Within moments the vent had opened, and music began playing inside of my head. I sat down on the bed, trimmed a lock off my hair as a slow hip hop beat could be heard building into my mind and carefully placed it in the envelope, setting it under my bed to place in the vent when I awoke. Strange times, these 'nights'. As I flicked off my light and got into some pajamas the transition from day to night was complete. I had been there for years yet I was still unsure of what to do when the work was done. Fully exhausted after the stimulants wore off, I usually decided to drink and think. In a different mood today, I ignored the heavy thinking and went light on the alcohol to speak with Ghostie, who was now moving to the beat, an outline of a fragile woman's body, dancing in my peripherals.

"Ghost," I started speaking through the buzz of alcohol. "You ever think about what The Company does with all of this shit?" I inquired, referring to all the movement, the emotion, and thought.

"Mood killer," she responded. We cursed at each other humorously for a moment.

"I'm bein' serious," I continued. "The Face Farm is still so foreign to me. We've been here for years; shouldn't we at least be given an idea of what to do when we start?" I asked.

"Don't call it that, and maybe us figuring it out is what they want," she responded. "What we are doing is obviously working, keep the routine up until we need to change it."

Goodnight, Ghost, I think, unsatisfied with her answer. I took another sip of tequila, the bottle was heavy in my hands without stimulants pumping through my veins. I pondered the purpose of the nasty little e-slugs, and wondered what they do with those little bits of energy they sapped from the room.

Time for bed, I thought, putting what was left of the alcohol into the vent and requesting the music to be turned off. Sleep was no easy feat with The Veil still moving inside my brain, automatically relaying information between Ghostie, The Veil, and myself to create tasks of the routine to be accomplished in the morning. Images of the faces of horrific creatures raced across the black vision of my closed eyes in a phenomenon I liked to refer to as a 'face tracer', while I created a strange framework of nightmarish instances and 'what if' scenarios to be harvested for plots and world building additions of mass-produced media. It was building a palpable fear inside my head, winding me up as I was winding down. Nothing it seemed was wasted at The Company. The alcohol I had found improved the situation, if only slightly relaxing my muscles.

In the last bit of 'night', The Veil lied dormant in my mind and around my body, creeping out of me and rising back up to the ceiling only as I slept. Ghostie picked a spot outside of my field of vision and entered a resting state to gather energy to serve the following day, every time I had tried to catch a glimpse of her, she woke and moved with incredible quickness. I let her rest. I began practices in impermeable thought, to communicate with Ghostie outside of The Veil's coverage. It was unnecessary, really, but a small amount of privacy was nice, and it was a good challenge for the requests department's thought interpreters. I thought of the sound of static from an old television and played that in my head, to occupy The Veil's connection to the requests department while simultaneously thinking a background thought to send to Ghostie. It seemed to work thus far, although they have cracked a couple of number codes I have thought of in the past. I was hopeful though, that something uncoded, unable to be studied over time, within my mental capacity may be used as a work around.

I tucked my right arm under my pillow, with my head sideways atop it, in the sleeper hold position until all feelings went dull. A lack of blood flow from sustained stimulant usage. I closed my eyes, continued to think about the e-slugs, and darkness enveloped my vision.

My eyes opened to the feeling of intense pressure on my head as if The Veil were trying to crush me, I felt cold, and was unable to move as I watched the diaphanous, limp copy of my own body raised above me. The extension of my feeling of touch rose with the copy me, and I yearned to have it brought back. A visual representation of energy from the emotional crucible was poured into the floating shell above me, I heard screaming inside my head, alongside high-pitched chimes and felt a cutting cold as though heat was just ripped out of my body. An uncomfortably thick wetness of sweat formed all over me. I watched as the shell, now full of emotional energy, fell slowly back down into myself, and I feel an anguish that was almost tangible in nature. My body unwillingly curled up like a spider crushed under immense weight.

Holy fuck that hurts, I think through the pain. *Please be a dream, please be a dream.*

The immense pain faded instantaneously as I woke to those lovely, ghostly hands covering my eyes. I turned and flailed my arm wildly to bring the blood back before craning my head upwards. I watched through those clear hands as The Veil descended upon me yet again.

Ouch. Fuck! I thought as the acidic heat of a devious e-slug's digital slime nearly burns my pectoral, I grabbed it and tried to crush it in my hand to no avail, my fingers passed through its physical form, and it landed plainly on my stomach, I rose frantically with the strange dream fresh in my mind, along with the sudden pain thanks to the e-slug, and pass through the horizontal plane of The Veil energy which delivered a decent electric shock to my entire body. I flopped back down on the bed, feeling chastened by own haste, and took a breath. I then carefully picked the e-slugs off while awaiting The Veil to take hold of me.

Feeling slightly defeated, I decided to skip the energy draining struggle against The Veil's melding. It began to take hold as I picked what was hopefully the last e-slug off my shoulder to frisbee it across the room.

"Please get off of me Ghostie, I'm not in the mood for this shit," I communicated seriously in my mind. The crescendo of response built into what sounded like laughter, though she did remove her hands from me. I was not amused, but with the entire day ahead of me I didn't have time to complain.

I took off my PJs and threw them in the pile of e-slugs in the far point of the room, I had forgotten to send them off. *Whoops,* I thought, signaling the critters to go back to the reactor. While the e-slugs were slowly making their way to my ceiling light, I flicked it on, opened the vent and delivered my enveloped lock of hair, then grabbed the stimulant tonic and downed it before throwing the same jeans and hoodie on from the day before, which were now cleaned by The Veil energy. Feeling a bit more active with the drink digesting, Ghostie and I got to work, and I turned on the heater. We were guided by The Veil through easier moves of the routine again, and I was delighted to see some of the more memorable movements from yesterday, being expanded upon. I continued with some of the more difficult moves forming new movement patterns and collecting electronic shivers as substantial heat was building up around me. With The Veil guiding me through the static body glove to a seated position on the bed I knew it was time for the roulette-esque emotional crucible. My discomfort at the crucible's recent intensity must have been noticeable as I could make out 'don't be a pussy' coming from the ghost to my left.

A stabbing pain could be felt in my spinning guts and a heavy strain in my head and chest making my breathing stifled, and my now upset stomach reeled in newly discovered ways. I turned cold despite the heat in the room, and I fell to the floor, gasping for little bits of air here and there. I endured, and the sharp stabbing pain evolved into a blunted, but heavy weight in my gut, and an unwelcome tickling in the back of my throat, making muscles clench and forcing me to dry heave over and over, my throat and stomach unsatisfied with not being able to produce anything but thick spit and stomach acid. This continued until streams of tears fell from my eyes, and I could feel myself slipping from consciousness while deep in sick agony. Then, nothing. I found air for my lungs, and the gross, sickly feeling in my gut was gone. The Veil wiped away my tears as a mighty electric shiver was felt throughout the entirety of my body.

"See, that wasn't so bad," said the ghost inside my head.

"*Fuck yourself Ghostie*," I replied mentally, relieved that the experience was over.

"You've cried twice in two days," she started through laughter, which in turn made me start laughing, finding humor in the strange event. The vent opened and a short memo was inside. 'Upgrades to the crucible, sorry about the e-slugs' it read, which added to our humor.

Always on the move, I gathered myself to find my legs again, and ask Ghostie, "What's next?" Still feeling cold I turned the heater up a click.

"Freestyles," she responded. I mentally requested a large bottle of red wine and picked it out of the vent moments later.

"Third party viewing test," Ghostie communicated as I took a swig from the dark glass bottle. While standing, I closed my eyes and stretched my imagination to view myself from Ghostie's perspective, raised my right hand, and matched what I was doing in the image being created in real time. I stood on one foot, using the slight heaviness of Veil energy that surrounds me as type of counterweight to keep my balance, and viewed myself doing so with Ghostie's eyes. My eyes closed I could feel her move in front of me and the perspective of myself shifted with her. I was looking at my eyes, through hers, and her vision was bright even through my closed lids. The thought of opening my eyes to catch a glimpse of her phantasmal body enters my mind.

"Don't do it, remember what happened last time," she warns as the mental image of third person viewing in my mind collapsed to a blank slate, I kept my eyes closed.

Last time I saw your beautiful face I was blasted and blinded by intense light form energy you put off as our eyes made contact, left thinking I saw God and having to move in the dark for two days with my brain scrambled, guided only by the sound of your voice, and the touch of Veil, I thought, still debating whether it would be worth it to try again, with some sunglasses on.

"Yeah, that was a slow week," she responded dryly. We finished with the third-party viewing test as I took a big gulp of wine and turned the heater up a click. My room was becoming satisfyingly tropical.

The Veil and The Company remained ever mysterious to me, giving hints, and leaving me mental glimpses that allowed for some insight to the work being done creating something so much larger than a just a person feeling, thinking, and moving in a sealed room. There was a type of trust between us established after many mental breaks and bodily injuries, and as mysterious as The Company was, they had decided to listen and change methods of labor, working within my mind and working with my mind to create something better as the technology advanced and evolved over the years. I had been able to evolve with it. They always cared and I always decided to continue through instances of doubt and fear. Now the job was nearly done.

These previous years I had learned to enjoy exercises in freestyle thought and bodily movement, it was a chance to lend expression, nuance, and a bit of experience from my life to what is being created behind the curtain of The Veil, which has transformed from the early days of strict routine and monster creation to something more tangible, artistic, beautiful, and maybe a bit glorified in my eyes. Some movements we created were laced with a bit of experience from my life before being employed by The Company; sports, math, science, all manners of activity had lent an understanding to my muscles' balance in this specific body, making some movement look practiced, and others a bit more awkward. I found myself a blank page to ways of thinking and dialogue, not understanding of political differences, a tendency to build framework of empathy, and understanding rather than speaking on my indifferences towards them. It was easier in this sealed room, free of influence and the complexity of social interaction other than that with a ghost and schedule, to enjoy thoughts as they come, and despite the room's emptiness, I somehow always had something with which to occupy myself. I also enjoyed the creation of these monsters and creatures because I understood their purpose, to be horrific. To scare and frighten an audience. Now that the job has become more than that, I could feel myself becoming more as well. It was a simple give and take and simplicity was monumental to me. I supposed that's how the job started, refining things of nuanced, and intricate nature to create simplicity. We continued.

"Ghost. What's ne—" I asked in thought, with eyes wide open, interrupted as the entire room proceeded to flicker a single time with darkness, I looked upwards to see my ceiling light still on, left wondering if I had blinked unknowingly, not likely in the self-conscious state I had just been performing in.

I shook the eerie feeling off thinking of 'big shadow' projectors from past ventures as Ghostie responds, "Deaths, shot through the heart."

I drank a bit more of the wine, saving the rest for down time. I moved away from the bed, standing, and as Ghostie whispered, "Bang." The Veil would send sharp stabbing pains into muscle groups adding realism to my reaction, and I would slump over onto the floor, hands clenching my imaginary wounds, then reset, and repeat the process, with different areas of my body being targeted.

"Bang," she would say, as I pretended to bleed out on the floor, letting my body go limp and squeezing the air out of my lungs, staying still for as many seconds as I could muster before drawing breath again and standing to reset. My imagination drifted to a Western-like montage of nameless thugs brought down in hails of gunfire, what The Company would do with these moments I could only imagine. We continued for a couple of hours like this.

"Bang," she communicated, and I crumpled to the floor. Reaching out, I crawled to the bed, to 'die' one last time as she advised.

"One more… A short one but a tough one."

"Tell it to me straight doc," I jested through the building heat.

To which she replied, "Take a break."

I thought about it for a few seconds.

Damn it. All right, I thought as I stood up, my right arm being guided into position, pulled straight back away from my body and locked into place, yet the feeling of it being extended past the point of the joint's physical capabilities continued and I could feel phantom ligaments and bones fighting the strain, I winced and grimaced against the massive pain in my elbow and shoulder, until an audible snap! Was inserted into my mind, my arm went numb, and I fell to the bed, holding the limb with my other hand until the feeling began to come back and the counterfeit aches disappeared.

I turned the heater off after we finished, the room absolutely sweltering. I sat down and polished off what was left of the wine, to counteract what was left of the stimulants coursing through me.

"Ghostie?" I asked, deciding to try my luck in impermeable thought as The Veil wiped beads of sweat from my face and body. I used the technique to request another bottle of wine. The vent opened shortly after with a memo inside reading 'Unintelligible'. With a bit more confidence in the method I asked the ghost.

"How did you come to exist?" Over the years I had formed a myriad of theories, about the work, the mystery of The Company, The Veil, the adventures, and Ghostie too, when she arrived. I had thoughts of asking about my spectral partner, but as our crude communication evolved over the years, and most of my questions asked, both vague and direct, were left unanswered, I decided to turn my attention to the work, as I often did. I heard a bleak seriousness in the spirit's whisper.

"Death. Within The Veil. Which once knew me as it now knows you." I was surprised to 'hear' her mimicking my mental encryption, and I noticed her sudden seriousness, which felt out of place outside of the routine. The chance of death within The Veil had occurred to me before, now knowing it was something that was indeed possible, I shuddered without the help of an electronic shiver. My head was now brimming with theories on how Ghostie had come into existence. Did her death leave mass data imprints on The Veil technology or was her presence more akin to the anchorage of the human soul to energy, after physical demise? Much room to speculate, and speculate I must, unsure of how long my practice in impermeable thought could go on and lacking in the total confidence that it had worked at all, I had to let it be.

I requested a continuation of the musical playlist from the day before, and a small glass beaker with a lid, minutes later the Vent opened, and I had it in my hands. I replaced the now empty wine bottle and closed the vent. I gathered a large amount of spit in my mouth and let it fall past my lips into the glass container, proceeded to seal it, and positioned it underneath my bed for tomorrow morning.

Still feeling a bit wired from the stimulants from earlier today, and with a bit of heat in the room, I was

33

uncomfortable with laying down for sleep at the time and my chest still had an itchy burn from the touch of the e-slug earlier today.

"Ghostie," I communicated now allowing The Veil to listen.

"Let's talk."

"About what?" she replied,

"Theory on the abstinence of artistic works before the entering The Veil."

"Palette cleansing?" She responded, referring to the six-month departure period of all forms of media before entering adventures within The Veil. No television, video games, electronic experiences, news, or books are allowed before the process begins, turning the mind sterile.

"Does the theory hold any truth so far?" I asked.

"Plausibly. We still find bits and pieces of media influencing your mind from years back, but those may be necessary to maintain creative thought and be built upon as framework for new avenues of creativity. We have been moving forward with some of those elements in mind. I doubt the palette cleansing process serves as much more than a light retraining of the mind, to deter outright copying from taking place. I know of a whole department of movers dedicated to doing old things in new ways, so I wouldn't place much thought to it." Satisfied having a couple questions unearthed and answered, I decide to lie down and let the three-way automatic communication take place, to create a schedule for tomorrow.

With the sleeper hold in place and the heat of the room dissipating I still found myself unable to chase down sleep. Thoughts moving between the three of us as one continued on for what felt like an eternity, and even without feeling the stimulants any more, it was making my body fidgety. I switched arms and kicked my legs out in various positions searching for comfort that could not be found. I sensed energy outside of my body, a sixth sense like activation of being watched beyond what I was already accustomed to in the room, slightly melancholic. "Ghostie, you feel that?" I spoke in a whisper, and scanned the room, finding nothing but the ghost moving alongside my field of vision. "No, go to sleep.," she responded plainly. I lied awake for what must have been an hour before returning to the sleeper hold and finding darkness.

I could not open my eyes, a mask of The Veil felt locking my face into a contorted visage, I begin struggling with my own breath, hearing a single distortion of a word I cannot comprehend come choking out from inside my mouth. The familiar feelings of how The Company received the moniker of The Face Farm, boiled over inside of me.

No more, I thought half-angrily, half pleadingly, with hopes of being awoken soon. *Come on Ghostie.*

I found air for my lungs, opened my eyes, and listened to the unusual sounds of ghost hands drumming on my back. Unsure of how much resting was done, I quickly build blood back into my arm and turned to field the incoming e-slugs, catching one right in the mouth, the static slime numbing my teeth and tongue, I nearly began to dry heave once again, picking it from my face and spitting with force before a grabbing the slug for a somewhat restrained lob across the room.

Positively sickening, I think as I arced one of the remaining slugs up to the ceiling to see if it would stick. It fell and landed in the pile with a meaty splat. They collectively made an audible buzz as though teeming with veiled energy. I walk over to the pile of them, request the vent to be open, picked one of them up and flung one of the maggot-like beings into the vent for study and data collection. The Veil's energy now within me as well, and with the recent breakthroughs in communication on my mind I decided to try something new with the e-slugs.

"Why here?" Using simple words in hopes of gaining a rudimentary connection with them. Staticky whispers of a collection of voices formed in unfamiliar tones.

"Why here?" I asked again, and with feedback reduced I make out what I thought were the repeated words.

"For I."

"For I, what?" I asked, yet they refused to answer any more questions and began making their way back to the ceiling light they spawned from.

I delivered my beaker full of saliva to the vent, trading it for a day's worth of stimulants, and pounded them. Despite the lingering feeling of a presence in the room, Ghostie and I proceeded chasing down electric shivers to The Veil's routine, which seemed to finish quickly.

The emotional crucible was an experience of dire weariness. My eyelids felt a sudden stiff bulkiness, my body the same, like I was being pulled to the earth. I picked at my eyes, fought to stand, and to stay awake. My heartbeat slowed even through the stimulants in my body, I dropped to my knees, and squeezed heavy air in and out of my lungs, fighting to not pass out for a good minute or two, I collapsed to the ground bordering on unconsciousness for another long moment, using all my physical strength to keep my limbs moving, and keep my eyes open. The sore heaviness lifted. A powerful electric shiver jolted me back to a sharp mindfulness and I was able to stand again.

With the heat up, stimulants in me, three beers out of the six pack I requested, and a few hours of mental freestyles under my belt, I began thinking back to when communication with Ghostie was nearly as basic as it was with the e-slugs earlier and recalled one of the mental exercises used over the past years to aid in the groundwork of understanding each other: "The multiple meanings of vocalized words with and without written or visual reference." The building blocks of established English communication between Ghostie, The Veil, and I. The words 'For I' still fresh in my mind I mentally requested a pen and a notepad to write down all combinations and ways to form these words out aloud. With notepad and pen in hand I began to combine the sounds and words, with an understanding that the slugs were pulling from my own vocabulary, and they were as follows 'for, four, fore, or, oar, rye, aye, I and eye' was what I could come up with, finding small humor in the words 'four eye' before delving deeper into the possible meanings. The pictured primitive nature of the e-slugs led me to believe that the simplest connection formed was more likely to be what was meant, which left 'For, four, I, and eye'. I then took those possibilities and began to speculate on potential meanings, 'For I'. *For I... what?* I thought. Were they referring to something I had done to them? I knew throwing them around the room was not harmful to the digital creatures. did this mean the energy is for themselves, or that the 'I' they were referring to was in fact myself and that I needed the energy in some way, or at least someone like me, unlikely with the fact that they harvest energy from my body as well as room when The Veil falls. Another mover perhaps? Were they in need of an energy source separate from The Veil? 'Four I'. Could there be four movers working on this or other projects that need something from the e-slugs? I never stopped to really count them as I picked them off my body, but there were for damn sure more than four of them. 'Four eye'. Something about my eyes and the eyes of Ghostie combined? 'For Eye'. Ghostie's strange eyes? Something about my eyes alone? They seemed to be working fine, did they somehow know I was blinded by Ghostie at one point? Or were the words shared between us simply misunderstood. When I privately questioned Ghostie about my findings I was met with laughter, a couple 'I thought we were done for the day', and a 'what the fuck are you talking about'? Finding the process more difficult without the slugs here to communicate with, I stopped. I returned the pad and pen to the vent. Satisfied with the mental hoops I just jumped through while uncovering the unsatisfying possibilities, I took an actual break, and with the room feeling like the inside of a furnace, I turned the heater completely off.

I sat down on the bed sipping on a beer waiting a moment for the ever-present feeling of being watched to dissipate. It would not. I asked the request department about it.

"You guys doing anything I'm not aware of?" A single word, 'No' formed in my mind so I decided to leave it alone. I requested some music and did my best to relax, discomfort building inside of me. As I debated on speaking with Ghostie a bit more, the entire room flickered once again, adding to my uneasiness. Unsure of what just happened, I decided to speak with her.

"Ghostie, did you see the lights shut off?" I asked.

"No… maybe the lights are going out?," she responded, sounding unsure. My mind sorted through the possibilities. I thought about how difficult it would be to try and finish the rest of our work in the dark. I thought about how we had no connection to the living world out there. We had been like this for years though, so I could not picture a weather storm taking out the power. I could, however, imagine an energy surge or the bulb in my ceiling light going out. I flicked the light switch off, mentally requested a replacement bulb, and moved my bed underneath the fixture. The bulb came, I grabbed it out of the vent and removed it from the box it came in. In hopes of seeing where The Veil comes down from, I twisted the light's glass cover off. To my disappointment I found no source of Veil tech, no tangible path to the reactor. Nothing but a metallic pan, the bulb and the bulb's receiver, I unscrewed the old glass bulb and replaced it with the new one, hopeful that this would solve the flickering. I put the glass cover back, returned my bed into its original place and carefully put the old bulb into the vent. With my thoughts drifting to tomorrow's collection, I requested a paper towel, and a zip-up plastic bag. Once in my hands I proceeded to blow my nose with the paper towel, fold it up, stuff it into the zip-up bag, zip it up, and placed it under my bed for the morning. To my dismay, the lights shuttered once more.

Feeling a small amount better with today's work done and the light replaced, I turned it off, welcoming the dull base lighting of the room. As I sat on the bed, I sipped on some of the beer I had saved. I remained fidgety. An idea formed. I requested a couple of aromatic candles and a lighter. Within minutes, the vent opened for me to receive them, this time without the warning memo. I placed both candles on the ground, removing their metallic caps, began igniting the wicks with the familiar lighter, and after a moment I could smell the beachy and fresh fragrance coming from the waxy cylinders. A few hours of this and a couple of beers later, I grew restless, I placed my pointer finger into some of the melted wax, retracted my hand from the flame and let the silky substance harden on my finger before smushing it between my pointer and thumb and putting it up to my nose. I smelled the now close and strong scent. Memories of a trip to the beach and the fun had there invaded my mind, almost allowing myself to forget about The Veil for a moment.

While feeling more at home and simultaneously homesick, I witnessed what I had been waiting for. The room flickered and masked even the unsteady orange light being cast by the candles. For half of a second, darkness had engulfed the room a single time. With fear once again growing inside of me, I blew the candles out, fumbling to replace their caps to suffocate the whisps of light grey smoke before it grew intrusive. The terrifying framework of what many things could be happening entered my mind, was there something wrong with my brain, my eyes? I mentally asked the requests department what was going on. For what was an eternity to me, within my mind, I conducted many theoretical instances of worse case scenarios, many leading to my demise or disfigurement, until the vent popped open, and produced a memo which read 'All good on our end'. I trembled.

"Ghostie, any thoughts on this shit?" I asked, my mind racing.

"I'm already a ghost, I think I'll be okay," she replied bluntly.

Fear plagued me through the night, and I grew cold without sleep as the cross connection between the three of us completed, forming a routine for the next day. I searched the room to find Ghostie resting and turned my eyes carefully away as to not wake her. The sudden turn of events left a bad taste in my mouth compared to the usual strangeness I have grown acclimated to. For the first time in many 'days' there was no rest to be found, the sleeper hold produced nothing, hours passed as my body kept insisting to move towards a comfort that wasn't there. Face tracers skittered across the vision of my closed eyes as I shifted into different positions, working myself up beyond my own patience. I got out of bed and stretched. The Veil still within and around me I decided to meditate, moving to the floor, and crossing my legs beneath me. I focused on my breathing, slowing it down, drawing in large, more meaningful amounts of air. Doing what I could to bring silence and stillness to a body and mind habituated with movement and flow. About half an hour in, I reached a semi relaxed state, and I was surprised to feel The Veil's hold loosening and lifting out from my body and ear canals. I decided not to try chasing down sleep 'tonight'. Hoping for better rest after the next schedule was done.

While still awake, my mind drifted from the meditative state to one of fear, to thoughts of fiendish creations from the past. I was without the powers of The Veil and its connection to the crucible of emotion to reign myself in, and outside the containment of a dream, my nightmares along with the intense feelings of loneliness became a reality, despite the worsening pangs in my subconscious telling me I was being watched. I found myself trapped in the smallness of my room and experiencing a stimulant and/or Veil withdrawal. I put my back to the wall looking for a corner in the round room, searching for Ghostie. The lights began steadily flickering off for half a second at a time, quickening to match the ever-growing pace of my heart. Figments were forming in my blurred vision. I sensed movement in the room, no sound, just movement all around me. Shadows began to slither. My vision began to fade.

I must have blacked out. *Fuck,* I thought as I felt the surprisingly powerful hands of my ghastly partner gripping and shaking my collar in a hasty attempt to wake me.

Still sitting up against the wall, I instinctively looked up to realize the cause of her fervor. The Veil closing in above me. Hurrying to recover I sprawled out as quickly as I could, back against the floor. Just in time to let The Veil work its way in. It did, and I felt immediate relief from the stressful night I had just endured. The crescendo of Ghostie's words began to build, she paused taking time for the connection to take hold.

"What the fuck happened last night?" she asked using the impermeable technique alongside a surprisingly loud volume in my head. I was slightly riled up, and spoke plainly.

"Not sure, couldn't sleep so I started meditating. I couldn't find you."

"Couldn't find me? I was right here all night," she said and gestured her hand up to the area opposite of where I had blacked out. My mind drifted.

"Hey, no e-slugs today?" I asked in my head. Normally I would feel relieved with the absence of the digital critters, but I was uneasy considering recent events.

"The Company probably cleaned them up," she said reassuringly.

"Or maybe they're full," I said.

"Yeah, full of your bullshit. Come on, we got work to do," she insisted.

"Fine, but something's goin' on around here," I warned.

Feeling a reluctance and a bit late for work I threw my staticky fresh attire on and got to it. I exchanged my bag of mucus for a bottle of stimulants of a new brand and flavor and swallowed the lot of it. My stomach was not used the new taste and level of carbonation. My guts lurched and felt like they folded in on themselves. Quick as I could I opened the vent to the garbage chute, and shamefully vomited up most of the stimulants into the garbage. Feeling a bit guilty at the unprofessional display, I requested another stimulant drink some disinfecting wipes, paper towels and another zip-up baggy. When they arrived, I then cleaned off the entire vent, neatly folding one of the paper towels now moist with bile into the sample bag and slid it under my bed for the next day. I sipped at the new chemical cocktail until my stomach settled and continued with the routine.

We finished the day's routine which I found again ended quickly, although quite difficult this time, I was unsure if it was due to lack of sleep or the off-brand stimulants still churning in my stomach. The room had flickered twice with a brief darkness already. The emotional crucible consisted of some type of abstract feelings that I could neither place, nor find words to describe. I sat on my bed, the truly sauna-esque, colossal temperature surrounding me. I turned off the heat and requested an ice cold mixed alcoholic beverage.

The words 'Anything specific'?

Asked in my head to which I responded out of exhaustion, "Surprise me."

Moments later a large, frosty glass of Long Island iced tea was produced, the request department even topped it off with a little umbrella. I laughed, slightly hysteric and as I sat down, I grabbed an ice cube to rub on my face and body. Between labored breaths I asked Ghostie if she wanted a sip of the tea. After she was done cursing me out, we conversed.

"Tell me what happened to you last night" she asked privately.

"I couldn't sleep, too wound up. The Veil left me after I calmed down. Nightmares took me. I was wide awake. Lights were wavering. I think I passed out. E-slugs might be feeding something. You know anything about it?" I replied chasing oxygen, keeping the conversation hopefully sequestered. She paused before replying,

"I remember my time as a mover, something came in from beyond the reactor, anchored me to The Veil, consumed my body."

"Any Idea what it was? Does The Company know?" I pried.

"Can't be sure, my memory of those days are limited. Something powerful, something dangerous I believe it was human, though, different. Perhaps we close our adventure here," she responded with that out of place seriousness. Calling it quits. I chewed on the thought. Nothing we had gained in terms of movement and artwork during all these days long past was at stake. I had seen the daily recordings from many of the great movers take place before me, with extensive records and data being sent to multiple locations and outlets across the nation. However, speaking on principle, my partner was dead, yet a part of her remained. What would happen to Ghostie if I were to suffer a similar fate.

"No, I won't allow that," speaking seriously myself for once. I faced the vent.

"Requests department?" I asked loudly, vocally, and raspy, finding my voice, long-lost through prolonged periods of silent learning and feats of patience.

"What are e-slugs?" I inquired, building up steam, surprising myself with my volume. The vent opened and a memo appeared, it read,

'Outliers within The Veil's digital body. They have been active until recently'. An anatomical diagram was forced into mental imagery, from which I learned they did in fact store energy.

"Did you see the lights flicker?"

The word 'No' appeared in my mind.

"Are there any beyond-digital formations other than the e-slugs, other than Ghostie and myself, other than The Veil energy?"

Moments later another memo appeared. It read: 'No, though we have been studying anomalous movement separate from the slugs. A patch of emptiness that The Veil moves around, but not through'.

"Where?" I asked aloud.

The words, 'it follows above you', appeared in my mind. I was hot.

"Were you fuckers going to tell us about this?"

One last memo appeared, it read: 'didn't want to alarm you'.

Now alarmed, I tried to cool down, and began processing the information I had. E-slugs appeared, gathering energy from the room, then disappeared. An anomaly moved above me. 'Following' me. Only I could see the lights wavering. An attempted connection with the mysterious being? Couldn't be sure, and I did not have any memories of a connection powerful enough to blot out vision, other than Ghostie herself which was more of a blinding light anyway. I was wary and weary. The work of the day, the new stimulants, the lack of proper sleep, the strange events, had all taken their toll on me. A fogginess could be felt building in my mind, and a dull heaviness in my muscles was growing. I dug at my eyes. The last thing I wanted to do was sleep. The three-way connection occurred and plans for tomorrow began to form, I fought to stay awake, yet my body found the bed, and while still in my jeans and hoodie, before I could move into the sleeper hold position, my eyes slammed shut, and darkness took me.

I did not dream. I woke to the sharp pain of having my arm pinched by the fingers of a spirit. My entire body was cold and wet, probably night sweats. My head was heavy and unclear, stuck in a bad case of brain fog, maybe the alcohol was getting to me. I flipped over to let The Veil do its thing. When it was done connecting with my mind, I felt better, but a lingering, heavy, dullness remained in my head, as though an intangible counterbalance was inside of it. It was difficult to move it the way I wanted to, it felt unnatural. My muscles were surprisingly sore, more than usual. My eyes felt itchy, as if somebody had thrown a fine dust into them, I picked and rubbed at them until the skin was sensitive and raw, and with eyes watering, decided I would leave the light off for now as I exchanged the bag of vomit for the stimulant drink which to my delight was of the original flavor, along with a small handwritten card that read 'An eye for an eye'.

Leaves the whole world blind, I thought, finishing the phrase. Unsure of the note's meaning and unfamiliar with the handwriting, I picked it from the vent and placed it under my bed. We began the routine and as the room warmed, my mind fog dissipated, my body felt relief, and even my eyes cleared up, though they still had a slight sting to them. Halfway through the routine I turned the light on, and as I endured the tremendous feelings of hatred and anger from the emotional crucible, darkness flashed in the room again, I caught movement just above my field of vision and looked up to see what appeared to be thick, untextured black ropes tapering to pointed ends, squirming with liveliness, up and into my ceiling light. The angers within me subsided swiftly, replaced by fear of the unknown. For the first time in a long time, I convinced Ghostie to stop the routine short.

"Ghost, how could you have missed that?" I asked, and theories began to form. Maybe she really didn't see it, her attention was on the routine, same as mine. The requests department said it wasn't picked up with any of their tech, a blank space moving within The Veil. The Veil, everything feeds off it, and Ghostie is anchored to it, maybe I'm the only one capable of seeing the creatures, being as I worked in conjunction with The Veil and my existence was not based on its energy alone. Maybe the creatures didn't feed directly off The Veil energy either, needing the digested and refined energy gathered by the e-slugs. I connected to the anomaly, or it connected to me, whatever it is. She responded,

"I'm not sure. I neither saw nor sensed any presence with us during the crucible phase. Although—"

"Although what?" I asked with heightened worry.

"—You have seemed a bit off these last couple days," she said.

I panicked, unsure of what those things were, figments maybe. The movement reminded me of a group of snakes writhing and wriggling in open space. The creatures, being not of my own, or at least deliberate creation disturbed me.

My immediate thoughts were of fear and danger, how to destroy them before they destroyed me. I knew that was not the correct mindset. I pushed past it, grasping for a comparison. Thoughts of Chester formed, a monster created with the intent of scaring, built to pull on feelings of fear and danger, emotions instilled in man from the dawn of their creation to aid survival. I thought of the snakelike creatures creating the anomaly. A snake is a dangerous animal under the right conditions and should be treated as such to avoid potential harm, the snake will do what it can to survive. I decided this was a more fitting way to think of the creature, or creatures, potentially dangerous beings, just trying to survive. To make a proper connection I needed to try with significant effort to understand, even through my monumental fear.

I requested a sterile pin, a plastic zip-up bag, a disinfecting wipe, bandage, and a tissue, which appeared in the vent sometime later. I took the items and sat on the bed. I then proceeded to prick the palm of my left hand with the needle, squeezed a small amount of blood with my other hand and then placed the tissue on the spot with light pressure. When the blood dried, I neatly folded up the tissue, placed it into the bag, zipped it up, and placed it under my bed for tomorrow, next to the handwritten note. I used the disinfecting wipe on the miniature wound, threw the wipe in the garbage chute and placed the bandage over the area.

With the lights off and my pajamas on, I sprawled out onto the bed. After hours of waiting and wondering what would play out during my next encounter with the anomaly, I decided to get some rest while I still could.

"You sure you want to continue this project?" Ghostic communicated.

I stifled a laugh.

"Fuck no! But that ain't stopping me."

I could feel the weariness taking me, but as I closed my eyes, shadows moved, a distortion of air like that above a bonfire, spreading throughout my room. I could feel the temperature drop a couple of degrees; something was approaching. Emotions of sadness entered my body, the feelings were impressive, but nowhere near crucible levels. E-slugs began raining from the ceiling, more than I had ever seen at once. The snakelike creatures made no sound as they quickly wriggled in from the ceiling light and flattened out against the ceiling itself, working together like a single being they strained, fighting for leverage. To my horror, a large oval like body began to protrude, shaking itself free from the digital reactor space, it then dropped to the middle of the room, altering The Veil's energy as it corrected itself in the air, the slithery creatures cushioning its landing. It turned towards me. I couldn't be sure if it was defying gravity or using the snake creatures that drooped to the ground to stand. My heart sank as I scanned sealed room trying to form an escape plan, but I knew there was no place to hide. The snakelike beings turned out to be part of a larger entity bordering the creatures' body. A gigantic human eye with top and bottom lids with enormous, wild, and thorned lashes. It was a picture of fatigue, looking uncomfortably jaundiced, a bit bloodshot and tiredly irritated. I watched as the e-slugs gathered below its body and climbed two outstretched lashes to deposit transformed Veil energy through contact. The empty husks of at least a dozen e-slugs fell to my floor and dissipated. The eye probed my mind for the foundations of a connection while I tried to collect myself. The optical extremity blinked a single time, casting a shadow of darkness through its closed field of vision. It used my brain to search for vocabulary and began making me speak gibberish in a choppy and strange manner. There was a time where I was accustomed to something similarly invasive back in the early days of The Company, but this creature took it to a whole new level of intrusion. I could feel it feeling me out as it slowly closed in on me, muscles spasmed in my arms, legs, stomach, and face. Its lashes lashed out, gripping at my head and face, thorns on the joints dug in, moving its mass behind me, and working its wet, slithering tendrils around my head and down my back. Air began being forced in and out of my lungs to an off-pace rhythm.

I quickly thought back to the communication formed with the e-slugs and mentally spoke out, but I could feel my thoughts being overwritten by the anomaly's powerful hold on me.

"Why here?" I asked mentally. I did not anticipate the strength of the headache I received as the creature picked words from my mind and forced them through my mouth. I sounded exhausted.

"Consumed energy…

Residual…

Found within the crucible…

Cold in the reactor…

So cold in the reactor…"

Impressed that it was able to pull from such varied dialogue, the range of powerful, mostly negative emotion held within the crucible and the pain of those many hours spent within it entered my mind. I now had hope that the monster I had built this eye to be in my mind was greater than the creature possessing me. I fought through the strange overlapping of thought to communicate with this creature.

"That's enough," I repeated until the entity responded.

"Can't go…

Need host…"

More concerned than ever I searched my room for Ghostie, struggling against the creature's control of my own eyes. I flicked them back and forth, straining them until they became watered and irate. I caught a whisp of her body moving within my peripherals. I managed to get a few words out, hoping she would receive the message.

"Ghostie, staring contest," I said with as much seriousness as I could muster.

My spectral companion turned and made indirect contact with my eyes. Even the ancillary light beams were akin to staring at two suns. The creature and I blinked rapidly in unison, I forced my eyes open while the entity continued blinking, casting darkness against Ghostie's bright whites, a strobing display. I could feel the anomaly's pain aching in my head and body, wriggling and reeling around me as my vision went white. I felt the spiny, sharp hold of the lashes on me loosen as I struggled to regain my control, hopeful that the indirect light would not be enough to blind me like last time. I was fully released, and I looked up to see a blur of the anomaly worming its way back through my ceiling light, up to the digital reactor.

"I still didn't see it, but The Veil's energy around you and the room was twisted. Darkened," Ghostie communicated. I sat next to my bed thinking the encounter over, with the lights on dim and newly acquired sunglasses on, sipping on some spiced and iced rum all thanks to the request department. The Veil energy felt more typical and was closing out the wounds on my back leaving impressively minimal scarring.

"Well, I did. It was a giant, tired, disembodied human eye, and I was losing myself to it before you came in. Did you hear it speaking through me?" I asked vocally.

"I heard you saying something about the crucible energy, and that the anomaly needed a host. One second. Hold still." Ghostie moved behind me and picked at the remaining open wound on my back. I winced through her efforts, but she worked quickly.

"The fuck is this thing?" she asked placing it in my hand, the object was clear as glass and hard as stone.

"One of the thorns on its eyelashes must have broken off inside of me." I mentally requested a sample bag and asked for the company to analyze the contents as I carefully placed it in the two-way vent. We continued.

"So, it sounds like it's been feeding on emotional, residual energies that soak the room. The e-slugs must have been gathering that energy, which was refined and emptied into the anomaly. Feeding it. It is strong enough to survive without the slugs now, though it needs me as a host. It comes in during sleeping hours, and possesses me, or at least hides in the room warming itself until it collects energy during crucible time then escapes back to the reactor."

"Where did it come from?" she asked.

"Can't be sure, I know it's not something we created, it felt like it could use original Face Farm techniques, maybe some surviving leftover from adventures of movers of the past, maybe something lived through The Veil's upgrades, limping on in a constant state of incompatibility."

"How can we kill this thing?" she asked.

"Should we kill it?" I asked.

"I mean I'm dead, I'm sure the eye will be okay," she replied.

"I disagree, and I think you might have a biased opinion on death. We can aid it. We can remove it from here and anchor it to an energy source more attuned to the anomalous frequency. It seemed to be suffering in the reactor."

"Also—" I started in impermeable thought, while showing Ghostie the card beneath my bed, reading, 'An eye for an eye'.

"—I think someone at The Company knows."

I spoke with the people of the requests department about my findings, they asked if I would like door installation to commence, ending my adventure early. I pushed for them to wait until the thorn's trace energy was analyzed. My heart was set on finding a more suitable home for the entity, and I could not allow other adventures to take place using this reactor, knowing the anomaly was potentially harmful.

"Well ghost. What shall we do?"

"Let's hold off on the routine for a while. Wait it out and see what the information the analysis brings us. In the meantime, we should try and get some rest," she replied.

I requested a large, sealable container, and some disinfecting wipes. Once they appeared in the vent, I told Ghostie to look away as I carefully urinated into it, not that I really had to go, but more to ensure everything was working properly, with it being months since my last urine sample. To my relief it was of a healthy color, I cleaned my hands with the disinfecting wipes and set the container beneath my bed for the next day's collection. I then threw myself onto the bed, locked myself into a sleeper hold and got comfortable, with a growing confidence that the anomaly wouldn't return tonight after being subjected to Ghostie's gaze.

I found myself trapped underwater, I held my breath as I dove down deeply, searching for something vague but important to me, it took a too much time to float back to the surface without air in my lungs, and I could feel a heavy burning in my chest and at the back of my head as my brain was screaming for oxygen.

I'm gonna die in here, I think as my adrenalin builds.

I awoke to Ghostie pressing repeatedly on my diaphragm pumping air back into me. I let out a long gasp, digging deep for air, must have turned on my back in my sleep. I kept my eyes closed to avoid eye contact with her, and as The Veil came down and melded to me, I gathered myself. Now in control of my airflow, I had to calm Ghostie down. Her thoughts crescendoed into my mind.

"Don't die on me now, you fuck!" Was on repeat with tones of worry and haste, once again surprising me with her volume. She may have saved me once again.

"Ghostie I'm fine. I'm fine," I said soothingly. She stopped pressing on me, her presence flew to my side, and I opened my eyes once I was safe, and she was in my peripherals.

"I'm all right, Ghostie, for real."

"That's up for debate," she said sourly, and I was glad to feel some bite back in her voice as it rang in my head.

I secured the container of urine from beneath my bed and delivered it to the vent. I decided I should take the stimulants from the vent even though we were off for the day. I requested a sour mixed drink and sat on the bed to speak with the ghost in my room.

"What do you think we're doing here ghost?" I asked.

"Creating something, and with recent events in mind, fixing something."

"Is that a good thing?"

"Good enough to keep you employed and my life force constant." I opened the vent to find a large margarita with shaved ice and began to sip it.

"You've been 'round longer than I have, Ghostie, what are your thoughts on the entity?"

"Thinking back to my death, I see you going through what I went through years ago. I know you want to continue the process and routine even through adversarial proposals. I am connected to you, tied to everything you are, everything you do. I'd like that to continue for as long as possible, see where the story ends just as I'm sure you would. The anomaly is a great danger to you, and by proxy me. I prefer existing, even in this stifled state, and I'm sure you would feel the same."

"Losing our connection isn't an option, Ghost, but I'd like to see this thing through."

The next day the requests department had finished analysis on the thorn. "Compatible with base level crucible energies of all varieties, sample deteriorates under strong ultraviolet frequencies of light." Not much to go on but better than nothing. I requested a can of spray paint and a reinstallation of the original emotional crucible, remembering it as a much softer experience, almost incomparable to the devastating waves of feeling put forth from the latest model. I also requested the development of an ultraviolet lantern.

Days went by as the requests department recreated the day one crucible, retrofitted to move within the current veil clouds. Free from the routine, Ghostie and I found ourselves speaking openly to each other, cursing, sharing stories of past adventures, our favorite parts of this one, playing games and laughing, uncaring of the ears of the requests department. Breaking out of the imagined shell of solitude and privacy we had been building around us for so long. The vent opened and both the UV lantern and red spray paint were now available, I placed the paint under my bed, told Ghostie to place herself in the farthest point of the room and set the metal cylinder to its lowest setting,

"I can't feel anything," she said. I turned it up one brightness level.

"I think I'm okay still." I flicked the switch on the lantern up to its maximum setting.

"I feel a bit warm but that's about it." Satisfied that the UV light would not harm Ghostie, I turned the lantern off to conserve its battery life and placed it under my bed.

"What are we going to name the entity?" I asked.

"You pick," she said.

"I named Chester, it's your turn," I replied.

"How about the Anomal-eye, no wait. The Outleyer," she replied.

"Outleyer it is."

Another couple days went by, the requests department notified us of their finished work on the retrofitted emotional crucible. I requested it to be hard pinned, centered underneath my ceiling light, which seemed to be the Outleyer's preferred entrance in and out of the room, and called for it to be imbued with soothing emotions of comfort and peace. I stepped into the area, and gentle feelings of solace washed over me.

This could work, I thought, as I turned the heater on its max setting, hoping to draw the Outleyer in.

"Now we just gotta wait."

Another day went by. I lied on the floor, with my shirt off and my jeans rolled up, sipping on a frosty mojito, and glanced at the heater, which had the room in an ungodly, torrid condition, made humid by the constant flow of sweat escaping my pores. It was a heavy heat. The Veil was hard at work wiping sweat off me. No lights were flickering, no feelings of being watched were present.

"Maybe we killed it," Ghostie communicated.

I licked at the sweat that dripped from my face before replying,

"It's possible, but even in the weakened state it was already in, the Outleyer was still so strong. Might just be scared of us now."

Ghostie and I withstood the slow cooker for a couple sleepless days and my body was beginning to reflect that. The daily dose of stimulants left my mouth feeling dry. I tongued at my lips now chapped and salty as I moved from my puddle of perspiration on the bed to create another on the floor, repeating this process until the requests department urged me to turn the heater down a couple clicks. I did. Even under the care of The Veil the heat was brutally taxing. I requested a towel to aid The Veil in wiping sweat off the floor and myself. The sudden drop in temperature along with the coolness of drying perspiration left me feeling a bit clammy. I decided it was time to call it a night. I threw my T-shirt back on and collapsed on to the bed. I turned my head to take one last look at the ceiling to see the contortion of sharp spiderlike limbs sprawl out from behind the light at the top of the room. I cursed softly and rolled off my bed to grab the spray paint. I sprang to my feet and emptied the can at the creature. *Fuck,* I thought as its skin began to absorb the paint. The room went blurred and black. The floodgates of adrenalin were broken open. I immediately felt the Outleyer connect to my mind, feelings of despair tore through me. I focused deeply to separate our thoughts. I forced words into my mind, *Brought you energy, trying to help you.* I drew air into my lungs and the creature forced it out, contorting my throat and mouth as I spoke.

"Too late…

No ghost…

Need host…"

I tried to yell out to Ghostie, but my mouth and mind would not cooperate. I felt I could reach out in impermeable thought, but I was slashed, whipped across my arm.. I could feel the wild, spiked lashes wrap and wriggle around it, I succumbed to instinct, turning my back to the creature with the ropes tight against my shoulder and hauled against the lofty weight of the entity, indifferent to the pain, high on adrenalin, and still feeling the effects of stimulants. I planted my feet looking for leverage and pulled with all my weight. I felt slight progress being made as my upper body dipped down. I reached out with my free hand, feeling the bed through the darkness in search of the UV lantern. I lowered my body, felt the paper card, approximated where I had the light hidden, and there it was. I gripped the metal cylinder, careful not to let it slip from my palm, still coated with a light sweat. I struggled to flick the switch on the lantern while maintaining my hold on it, unsure if I would be able to find it again if dropped. The Outleyer's hold on me was becoming more secure by the second, and its thorn covered lashes were digging in. The tightness of the grip began to crush the bones in my arm. My fingers in the locked-up hand went numb. Nothing the Veil couldn't fix. I fumbled at the cylinder with my other arm until I heard the click of the light, barely audible through the sound of my bones breaking, I turned back towards the creature, lantern on and in hand, and the entity released me immediately, my vision snapped back, I aimed the UV light more steadily following the creature as it once again started making an escape through my ceiling light. As it left, it took with it all thoughts of trying to save the godforsaken creature. Despite standing in the tranquil energy of the original crucible, I was boiling over and still wired. I was defeated a second time. My patience had run its course.

"Turn that goddamn crucible off. Ghostie, we're gonna kill this fuckin' thing."

Sleep waited as we prepared for war.

"Can we light it on fire?" Ghostie asked.

"Probably not the safest route for us to take in a closed room, we should consider that a last resort," I said adding a fifth of vodka, rags, a lighter, and a glass vial that should be easy enough to break with minimal force, to my growing list of requests. I sat sipping on a forty ouncer of generic beer in my good hand as The Veil painfully penetrated my arm to finish repairs on my battered limb. The requests department denied my demands for guns and ammunition, which were 'abolished in the turn of the century'. They did however, come through with a freshly sharpened knife bordering on the size of a machete that could barely fit through the vent, an equally sharp, foldable pocketknife, a light Kevlar jacket, pepper spray, quick drying adhesive, two weeks' worth of stimulants, half of a protein bar, extra batteries for the lantern and a dozen pieces of card stock paper which were numbered in large print. Each item was fed to me one by one through the vent, along with a memo that read, 'Are you sure you'd like to continue'?

The creature was invisible to everyone apart from me, and paint would not stain its body. I spoke with Ghostie about my plan to utilize her devastating vision while conserving her energy and without her needing to see the creature. Using the adhesive, I hung the papers along the wall in numerical order, evenly spaced one through twelve with a clock in mind. I sat on the bed with six at my back and twelve directly in front. I had Ghostie close her eyes and practice revolving around the room at a steady pace, waiting five seconds before moving from one number to the next. Once she was dialed into a roughly one minute revolution, and once I was able to keep track of her without visual cues, I began calling out numbers for her to fix her gaze on, based on her estimated, numbered positioning to create a straight beam of spectral light to that specific number while also making sure I had my back to her. It was a strange feeling to be the one giving callouts this time. I weighed my options. I thought of using mirrors instead of numbered papers but the likelihood of meeting Ghostie's eyes with mine in a reflection was too great. I tried the Kevlar jacket on, could be good against thorns and lashes. As light as it was it restricted movement. I took it off, folded it up and placed it back into the vent, opting for the invasive and painful, but quick healing of boundless Veiled energy alone. I found myself in deep contemplation over the nutrition bar, The Veil had always provided me with vitality and confident strength. My last substantial meal was beyond memory. A small amount of protein could prove useful if the fight were prolonged, but in the presence of Veiled energy I couldn't afford to risk cramps or complications of the stomach, I put the halved protein bar back in the vent, vying to stay hungry, stay light. I sipped on stimulants to remain vigilant. I sipped on the alcohol to remain warm and loose. I flicked the familiar lighter on and back off deciding to pocket it. I then soaked one of the rags in vodka, poured a good amount of the clear liquid into the glass vial, and stuffed the cloth halfway into it, thinking about how we might be flying blind in the upcoming battle. I turned the heater on, and we waited once more.

We suffered a sleepless night as one day blurred into the next, Ghostie and I practiced our techniques. Her timing as she revolved around the room was now immaculate. I quickly grew familiar with the weight and heft of the larger blade. I stuffed the smaller pocketknife into my jeans. As the hours in wait crawled by, figments began to form in my vision, twisting shadows and light into unholy geometry, apparitions seeming physical in nature came to me, I rejected the sights, having experienced them previously on this adventure. The figments developed as restfulness of the mind and body waned. Though harmless, they might complicate things. Ghostie decided to get some rest. I laid on the bed restless. That's what the Outleyer was waiting for, a moment of weakness. I grabbed the large knife and placed it next to me. I set the supply of stimulants next to the bed along with the lantern and pepper spray and waited for the effects of tonic I currently had in me to wear off. Hours later, I was slipping into a half-awake dream state, ignoring figments that shifted around in the dim lighting, I recognized the feeling of despair from earlier, along with the mounting sense of a presence in the room. I cracked an eye open to make out the shape of the Outleyer slinking down from my light onto the floor, its hazy image moved distorting the light. I requested veil energy to be hard pinned to my ceiling light to close the room off from the reactor. All three of us were trapped in here.

Ghostie it's here, I thought, reaching out with the impermeable method as I sprang up from the bed, putting me at six. I kept my sight on the creature while I indirectly watched her with great care as she moved with her eyes closed to *twelve.* I counted down the five second intervals between Ghostie's movement to the next number. The creature was centered in the room between us. My heart was thumping in my eardrums. I could feel the Outleyer's connection to my mind begin to take hold as Ghostie inched across the room to *one.* I hastily downed two bottles of stimulants. *Two.* It blinked once; darkness flashed into my vision. *Three.* A double dose of stimulants in me, I had time to think. My body was warm, and my blood ran cold. *Four.* The creature flicked a wiry lash towards me before planting it forward on the floor.

"A step in the wrong direction, you fuck." *Five.* I fought for space in my own mind as Ghostie moved beside me.

"Eleven," I said. Ghostie opened her eyes and fixated on the number, her gaze unrestrained, my mind was torn free from the pull of the Outleyer in a flash of intense light. It blinked violently and reeled in discomfort, casting pie shaped blackness across the room. I reached for the can of mace, taking a step forward to let Ghostie pass behind me. *Six.*

"Twelve," I said. I unloaded the can at the entity until my own eyes started to burn. I did not expect the substance to spread around the room so completely. I broke into heavy, uncontrollable tears, the Outleyer did the same. *Seven.*

"One," I said through my choking throat as I wiped at my eyes and searched through burning, watered vision for the UV lamp. I found it and switched it on as the Outleyer stretched out towards the ceiling unable to grip it through the thickness of Veiled energy. *Eight.* The creature was red with broken blood vessels and moved towards me unphased through the ultraviolet light with animalistic speed, flailing its thick thorny lashes with unhindered force. It drove a wedge between Ghostie and I, swiping the lantern from my hands and crushing it with familiar strength, leaving me at five and her at *Nine.* I produced the foldable blade from my pocket with my left hand, the Outleyer whipped at the hand holding it, thoroughly lacerating me. Stimulants in me, I made sure my grip did not fail again. *Ten.* The creature scooped me up in a thorny embrace. I swapped the knife to my dominant right hand and flicked it open. *Eleven.* I adjusted my grip on the blade and plunged the steel down on the abomination with force. It blinked sending darkness at me as I made contact. *Twelve.* Its skin was tougher than the thickest leathers, I sent the blade down repeatedly on the same area, viscous, crimson blood fortified with the heat of pepper spray spattered out from the small wound, nearly blinding me once more. The creature released me and wriggled backwards to be centered in the room again. I moved back to the bed returning to six. I wondered which of our eyes looked worse. *One.* The second skin of The Veil began to close to the gash across my hand. I was glad to see the Outleyer's small wound stay open. *Two.* I pocketed the folding knife in favor of the larger one sitting atop my bed. I watched how the Outleyer moved, shifting its weight, and slinking with its long limbs across the floor. *Three.* I shifted positioning from six to four as the eye turned to me.

"Nine," I told her. Light bathed the creature, which dampened the incoming lights in blinks of pitch blackness. With the eye occupied, I approached, stepping on one of the many long lashes it used as footing, and hacked it off with the long blade. Ghostie moved behind me to *four.*

"Ten." My body was blocking most of Ghostie's gaze, and I was able to cut through only a couple of the wiry appendages before it retaliated, whipping me numerous times across my stomach and chest. I took a step back. Deep cuts stained my skin with sticky blood. Stimulants in me, and adrenalin building, I pressed the attack. *Five.*

"Eleven." I stepped forward and jabbed at the bloodshot flesh but was deflected by the many defending lashes. *Six.* Ghostie was in my field of vision again.

I was soaked in sweat and blood. The smell of stale iron and body odor grew as the heat became a distressing factor. I did my best to keep the entity centered in the room, making the numbers more manageable and Ghostie blasted it with her gaze when the opportunity presented itself. This continued for what remained of the day, figments played with my vision as I struggled to hold my own against the creature. The Outleyer was stingy with its blood. I was losing good amounts of the red fluid from its counter attacks. The Veil sustained me. When I became weary, I fought back to my bed, and downed a day's worth of stimulants. I found as we fought, I was becoming hysterical, and struggled to stay aware of the count. I delivered a critical slash into the red and white area next to the iris, unprotected between lashes and lids. I requested a glass of whisky, which the requests department delivered in record time as the creature reeled in agony. I downed it uncaring as half of the burning liquid spilled down onto what was left of my clothing, stinging the plentiful cuts and gashes The Veil was tending to. I half-heartedly tossed the glass at the entity hoping the cup would fragment into shards and dust as it contacted the creature, but I missed it by a good amount. I stifled a laugh and got back to it.

Another few hours passed; I had drunk seven bottles of stimulants so far. The eye and I were looking ragged, blood splatter stained the entire room and small pools of it formed on the floor making the surface slick and slippery. My body was developing a legendary soreness and my mind slowed. Our battle was becoming an almighty lightshow, and my eyes were having difficulties with the constant adjustments. I had lost count of Ghostie's movement, stuck with continually moving my back to her when I caught her in my vision, relocating between attacks and looking at the numbers across from me to send her gaze at. My breath was labored, and I couldn't tell who was winning. My strength was wavering from blood loss and lack of rest. The heat in the room had me teetering between shock and stroke. The Veil sustained me.

I spat blood into the vent as a safety measure to ensure Veil synchronization continued. I focused on the creatures many remaining lashes, aimed at weakening its still substantial defense and movement. I did what damage I could before the Outleyer's wild counterattacks forced me to retreat. This continued for some time. Ghostie took the initiative of moving behind me to send a constant stream of light over my shoulders as I could no longer make out the numbers on the walls, which were distorted by figments shifting in my hazed vision. I was sure the creature was blind now, leaving its messy lashes in a protective pattern around it's closed lids, lashing out as it felt the thick, humid air being moved by my body. I was getting sluggish, I moved back to six, to my bed, and downed two more stimulant cocktails, fighting the acid in my stomach and at the back of my throat to keep them down. I did not know how long Ghostie could stay active while outputting constant light form energy from her eyes. The Veil sustained us.

Sometime later I could hear a large saw being started followed closely by a grinding noise. Door installation had commenced.

Not yet, I thought as I moved in hoping to end the Outleyer's life quickly. My attempt was sloppy. My calf was pierced deeply by a long lash, serrated with thorns. It slowly retracted the harpoon-like limb from my eviscerated flesh. I could barely feel the initial pain, numbed through the stimulants in me, but looking down at my leg which would not hold my weight, I collapsed, and the sharp agony of the wound finally registered. I lost hold of the knife from the sudden system shock, Ghostie closed her eyes, energy waning. I did not know what would happen to her if I died in here. The darkness the Outleyer cast swallowed the entire room, I crawled sending a deep pain from the wound in my leg. The Veiled energy penetrating the cavity burned worse than the damage itself. I was thankful for having the pain necessary to stay awake. I grabbed the lighter from my pocket. I flicked it on, placing my hand over the flame to ensure it was burning in the colorless, light consumed space. I reached out to her.

"Need you Ghostie, it's getting' dark out here."

I grabbed the makeshift Molotov from under my bed clumsily igniting it by way of feel and estimation. For once I was relieved the lights began to flicker. The incendiary was lit and Ghostie's vision cut a path of pure light directly through the encroaching darkness, revealing the Outleyer. I stole one last look, partly to admire the tremendous strength and prowess of the strange creature, mostly to gauge distance. I collected all my remaining stamina to aim from a seated position on the floor, and lasered the lit mixture home. Glass shattered, fire spread, darkness lifted, my day was done. I watched as the Outleyer sizzled and popped, consumed by flames until it fell to the floor becoming a still pile of smoking flesh in the puddles of drying blood. The smell was outrageous. I was unsure if I imagined Ghostie saying, "I fucking told you." I passed out from overexertion.

When I awoke days later, I was feeling much better, but unsure if any of the damage, either physical or mental would be permanent. My clothes were changed, and my body was washed of sweat and blood. I was tired, suffering from severe stimulant withdrawal, and I could tell The Veil was keeping my sick stomach at bay. I was in the same room, now at a comfortable temperature, the creature was gone, and Veiled energy could be felt finishing the therapeutics on my mind, stomach, and muscles, but I couldn't find her. I reached out with my mind. Ghostie was gone. I ignored the many smiling faces in suits and lab coats gathering around me and reached out to her in my mind. Nothing. I panicked.

"Ghostie where are you, Ghostie tell me you're okay!" I shouted.

"Mover," one of the suited women said with a smile. Her voice jolted me, loud and clear without static feedback.

"She's right here."

"Show me please," I responded, slightly soothed by her confidence and smile. She reached into her pocket and put forth a small steel device that looked similar to an antique style pocket telephone.

"What exactly do you mean, where is she?"

"It's been years, Veil technology has been advancing steadily. She is still affixed to you." The woman pressed one of the buttons on the apparatus. The mixture of hard light and veiled mist created the form of a woman before me. It was her, Ghostie, more solid, more tangible than ever, she looked real. I felt immediately connected to her, surprised at how painless the process was. I didn't care if I was blinded for days. I looked her in the face, eyes wide open, her eyes like extra bright lightbulbs, less blinding by a large margin. I kept staring for a long time. She was beautiful to me.

"Ghostie, how are you?" I asked.

"I feel better than ever. You look like shit though," she responded loudly and clearly through the device.

"That's my fucking girl!" I said excitedly fighting back tears. I slapped her outstretched hand with all my strength and a sobering, thunderous pop rang out. I tried to hug her, but she shifted her physical properties and allowed me to pass through her once more.

"We've got a lot to discuss," said the woman as she passed me the device and helped me to my feet.

"Tomorrow," I said.

"No, we need to debrief you on this adventure," she insisted.

"Tomorrow. Please give me a day to rest and process everything. I'll be in a better mindset tomorrow," I continued, hoping to get the hell out of the room asap.

"I understand, but we cannot let you leave, you can have your pick of rooms to stay in," she said.

"Can we go outside for a minute? I have questions," I added. The growing number of unrecognizable people flowing into the small room began to wear on me.

"Of course," the woman replied, and we started to make our way out of the room. People began to crowd Ghostie, the woman and myself. They asked about things and told me things. I could not discern the voices individually, though they all seemed encouraging and upbeat about what took place here. My claustrophobia had been building over the last couple of months and its peak was near. I could feel the connection to the requests department had been severed from my mind, while my connection with Ghostie was stronger than ever.

Ghostie, staring contest, I thought. I watched with a small amount of pleasure as every person in her field of vision, apart from the woman we were walking with was stunned by veiled light from Ghostie's eyes, carving a path for us.

The three of us exited the room. This was big for me. The air felt cool and fresh. The room seemed more massive in scale than when I had entered long ago, the ceiling stretched to the floor above this one. Everything was larger, and more real than I had remembered it. I glanced at the entrance to the storage room, bar separated by the vents, and the windows into the computer laboratory, everything looked unfamiliar from this point of view, different from what I had pictured deep in my memory. I broke from the party, delighted to see the bartender I once knew, still in proper attire and now on the precipice of being an elderly gentleman. He appeared to be the same person from years past that made me many memorable beverages before I first entered the room, though I did not remember his name.

"The barman is fine, and this is indeed cause for celebration," he spoke, eerily finishing my thoughts and smiling. Without my asking he removed himself from the bar's keyboard and monitor and produced a mixed drink from behind the bar. I sipped it and found it was the same cocktail as from the day I started the journey.

"This is fantastic barman, thank you for everything," I said genuinely as we embraced each other, I felt like I may have overworked this man over the years. The suited woman grabbed my arm and pulled me towards the hall.

"These people know you deeply. As do I," the woman said as we walked to the elevators my drink still in hand. We chatted with each other freely as we rode the elevator to the building's lobby. We stepped outside and exited the structure out into the large courtyard. I watched as movers, suits, and a surprisingly skimp amount of security guards spoke with one another walking to their destinations within the citadel. It was true daytime, and a sprinkling of rain drizzled upon us from the light cloud covering in the sky. I looked upwards in astonishment of the massive atmosphere and towering buildings set before me. I glanced back to the door we had exited, and my eyes rose upwards following the features of the unending towers piercing the clouds that Ghostie and I had called home for eight years. They were intimidating I thought as I sipped the mixed drink, attempting to settle my stomach. I was about to ask what year it was when the woman began speaking quickly.

"We are still processing your work. You are no longer connected to that room's Veil reactor. The year is 2203. Most of your original crew had abandoned the project. We were barely able to track Ghostie, let alone understand her when she first joined you, everyone can see and understand her with the help of the new device. We could not visualize your Outleyer at all. We genuinely thought you were going insane until you presented the thorn to us. As far as that anomaly goes, we are doing studies on its anatomy right now, we do not know of its origin. We have seen everything you have done, and no, there were no cameras in the room. We have followed you and Ghostie through the eyes and data structures of The Veil alone. You have discovered some new methods through your solitude. In fact, you have topped the mover's leaderboard for the past two years consecutively, though not by much. You will be overtaken this year due to your run in with the anomaly. The Company has expanded rapidly through knowledge sharing between movers and request departments." She took a second to admire Ghostie.

"And though you have several unique qualities you were not the sole factor to our success. We know you do not want another mover participating in an adventure like yours. We agree that it would be far too dangerous until your old reactor has been thoroughly reworked and upgraded. We were watching you with great interest, seeing how far you were willing to take your outdated contract and old-fashioned technology. You were extremely close to finishing the agreement with us, and through multiple demands both internal and external we have decided to close your contract as completed. The discussed amount has been deposited into your account. It was by far worthwhile to us, though you're wondering whether it was worth it to you," she said, stealing the answers to the questions that formed in my mind. More questions formed, I had to ask her to stop as her predictions of our prerouted conversation were making me uncomfortable.

"It's been eight years," I said.

"You've only aged three," she replied.

"How old does that make me?" I asked, ashamed to be unaware of my own age.

"You're thirty-nine years old though your face and body will not reflect that with how much time you've spent in the presence of Veiled energy over the years," she said.

"And Ghostie?" I asked.

"That's private you fuck," Ghostie interjected with refreshing pronunciation and audible clarity.

"Was that the same thing that consumed and killed her?" I asked motioning towards Ghostie.

"We don't believe so. Anomalies were more frequent in the early days," she said.

"I thought I was a part of the early days," I protested.

"You were as far as accessible records go," she stated.

"What is your name?" I asked.

"We know you don't like to do names," she said.

"I can learn," I replied.

The suited woman led Ghostie and I to our room high within the citadel housing section, a couple building across from our original workroom which had hotellike qualities that I found comforting and spacious. She handed me a business card with hers and other various telephone numbers on it. I locked the door behind her as she departed. I scanned the room, separate queen beds divided by a nightstand, and a large, clear glass television hung opposing the beds over a dresser. On top of the dresser, I found several devices for electronic experiences. I turned the monitor on and set the volume on low for some background noise, trying to adjust my ears to a world without feedback and the sound of static. Severe hunger and thirst hit me. I mentally requested a litany of my favorite foods, fruit juices, and sodas. After about twenty minutes of no response or knocks at the door, I realized I wasn't connected to the requests department any more. I stared at the room's phone for a long time trying to remember how to work the device. I produced the card the suited woman had given me and found the number for room service. I slowly, and with great care punched the numbers in. They quickly picked up and asked what they could do for me. I didn't know how to respond and was startled by the volume and clarity of the other end. I hung up without speaking a word and took a breather. I realized my stomach, after months without sustenance wouldn't be able to hold all the foods that had been painting my imagination. After a few moments of psyching myself up

I had enough confidence to redial. I ordered some buttered toast, a couple pieces of bacon, and some grape juice. After ordering Ghostie and I explored the room, we were excited to find a deck of cards on the nightstand. I practiced my shuffling techniques as we played go fish and waited for the food to arrive.

"What are you going to do with all that money?" Ghostie asked.

"What are we going to do?" I asked. I paused having not really considered it. Money was not the reason I became a mover, though paper had its perks.

"Maybe I'll take you out on a date," I said only half-joking. The food arrived. I picked the plate and cup from the hands of room service. I placed the ceramic on the bed and the cup on the nightstand. I ensured Ghostie was occupied with the television before I laid on the bed and stared at the feast set before me, smelling the melted butter and the aroma of the thick cut bacon until I could not contain my hunger any longer. I ate and sipped the juice while constantly reminding myself of my mother's words to me long ago to, 'slow down and enjoy your food'.

"How is it?" Ghostie asked.

"It's all right," I said hoping she wouldn't be upset with me partaking in subtle decadence. There was half of a piece of toast left on the plate when I was done. I felt full and satisfied. True nightfall came and I was suitably tired. I asked Ghostie what the battery life on her portable Veil device read.

"Due for recharge after 5.5 years of constant use," she said from the bed beside mine.

"Better plug it in tonight just to be sure," I said as I began to connect the appropriate wires. I kicked off the new shoes I had awoken in and placed them under my bed. I stretched for a few long minutes, spread out on the uncomfortably comfortable bed, and closed my eyes, unsure and uncaring of what to expect from my dreams or the following day. Despite my separation from The Veil, face tracers remained, and I had to continuously stop myself from planning tomorrow's routine. I was able to sleep easily after I had calmed my mind, no sleeper holds necessary.

I was standing outside, lost, viewing myself as my mind's eye drifted away, zooming backwards towards space. I watched as the speck I had become disappeared quickly into the mass of the earth surrounding me. I wanted to move forward, to move back to myself. I kept moving backwards, and the size of the earth itself and everything in it quickly became small too.

I had awoken, I felt sticky with sweat. I was awake and Ghostie wasn't beating on me. The sun was shining through the window, and she was soaking in the view. I looked up and braced for The Veil's arrival. It just was not there. I had to urinate to the point I felt my bladder would burst. I crawled out of bed and made my way to the bathroom to take care of it. I looked around, found myself in the mirror, The Veil had healed my physical damage and only a few slight scars remained. I didn't really look much older than eight years prior, though my hair had become a bit wild for my liking. I put my hand on the towels that were stacked neatly on the sink. Soft. I turned the shower on, it had been years since I had seen touched or tasted water apart from the ice diluting my beverages. I put my hand in the liquid that cascaded from the showerhead. Too hot, I cranked the handle in the opposite direction. Too cold. I debated skipping the shower. No, I must. I fiddled with the handle for a few minutes, until I had finally found the correct warmth. I reminded myself to take my clothes off before I commenced bathing. My skin was sensitive to the small fluctuations in temperature, and as I entered, the water nearly felt like The Veil's second skin. I washed with the provided soaps and liquids. I got out of the shower and wrapped myself in a towel before moving to the sink, where I found a miniature toothbrush and toothpaste. I brushed my teeth and enjoyed the freshness of the mint flavor that coated my mouth. I felt true cleanliness that The Veil had tried to copy over the years. I made my way to the dresser drawers, where I found the same brands of T-shirt, underwear, socks, and jeans that had been with me for so long. I put them all on, along with my brand-new shoes. "How're you doin' today Ghostie?" I said moving to the closet.

"Pretty good, still getting used to the upgrades. This Veil device allows for easier adjustment of hard light, increased physical interaction with the material world, a sense of touch, more control of light wavelength manipulation from my eyes and a learning emotional calculator! They aren't perfect but I have feelings again!" she exclaimed lifting the bed frame with one hand, sounding uncharacteristically loud and enthusiastic. I was about to give her the calm down motion with my hands but settled for raised eyebrows and a smile. She was delighted, leaving that room had been big for both of us, so all I could do was smile. My attention turned back to the closet, "Sweet!," I said with a bit of excitement myself as they had provided a hoodie in my size. I felt relieved as I put it on.

"What do we do now, Ghost?" I asked.

"Get your shit together and your thoughts in order," she responded, still loud.

There was a knock at the door, I unlocked and opened it and the suited woman entered with a stack of papers of almost biblical thickness. "Good morning mover. Good morning Ghostie," she said with that familiar smile, as she laid the hefty stack of paper and a pen on the bed.

"What's all this?" I asked, already knowing what it was.

"We want to know everything from your perspective leading up to and including your encounters with the Outleyer," she said.

"I thought you had recorded everything with The Veil technology," I said.

That's like eight years' worth of reports, I thought with disdain.

"Pay attention, dumbass," Ghostie responded aloud, through the Veil device. We all looked at each other in an awkward moment. The suited woman continued.

"We did, this is more of an assessment of you, what you've learned and what your thoughts on the project were, how it started, how it ended, and where you're at now that the project has closed. Contact me when this is completed. We're hoping you'll have it done within the month," said the suited woman as she left the room.

"Better get to it then," I said to Ghostie with a sigh. The pen didn't work.

Two weeks went by, we found ourselves stuck in a room again. I proceeded to build a new routine, one of cleanliness, brushing my teeth and taking a long shower before changing into freshly washed clothing. I became well acquainted to room service and television. Ghostie and I traded information of our individual outlooks on what took place. Filling out forms with questions not limited to our daily workloads, philosophies, injuries, traumas, downtime, drug use histories, past relationships, experiences, everything about our lives both related and not related to our involvement in the sealed room. We checked boxes and were prompted to write things, from summaries, lengthy and brief, to essays on whatever topic and parameters The Company called for.

"I can't believe they're making the dead do paperwork," Ghostie said.

I was readjusting to my body's original settings. I found my mind foggy, and body aching in stimulant deprivation and Veil overexposure. On top of the paperwork, I was constantly hungry, thirsty, or in need of a bathroom break, all of which felt foreign to me. I was developing new patience with myself.

Is this how people feel all the time? I thought.

"The perks of being digital," Ghostie said, digging at me. I ignored her. I continued whittling down the papers until I turned to find pages on personal motivations. I stared at them for a few long moments.

"I'm done for now," I said as night came.

I gathered the small remainders of our paperwork and placed it on the nightstand. We rested on our beds and turned our attention to the television. Ghostie had the remote, and flipped through the expansive horror film selections, though nothing was immediately recognizable as work of ours.

"How about *Death in the Depths?*" she asked. The title alone made me panic and constricted my breath. I was wishing she would pick anything but underwater material. I took a moment to think about it.

"Hell yeah," I said deciding it would be a fitting distraction.

In the morning, we finished our meticulous walkthrough of what transpired in the room. I dialed the suited woman's number, and she picked up; she was elated to hear that the files were complete and said she would be meet with us the next day.

"What do you think is next, Ghost? Suits and handshakes?" I asked.

"More likely lab coats and exams," she replied.

"I think I'd prefer that anyways," I said as a knock was heard at our door. I looked through the magnified hole in the door and unlocked it. Room house cleaners came in asking for dirty clothing and some time to clean.

"Let's go for a walk," I said with an urge to stretch my legs. I unplugged the Veil device and pocketed it. "How about we assess your range," I said as I made my way to one end of the long hallway and put my back to the wall. Ghostie left my side and walked slowly, distancing herself the length of our original work room, and stopping.

"Here we go!" she exclaimed, sounding unsure. She made it another room length, and another until she was halfway down the long hallway, she kept going until she reached the other side, and her image began to waver. I spoke to her mentally, and aloud to the device with no response. My mind was going off to worst-case scenarios filled with fear of losing her and I was unsure of how much farther we could push it without her consciousness deteriorating, so I quickly made my way back to her.

"Pretty impressive," I said with a smile.

"I feel like that was close to the limit," she said.

We went back to the room and my mind was reaching out in attempts to predict the day ahead. We turned the TV on once again to consume the ever present, readily available shows and movies. I was lost in thought with knowledge I had buried long ago in my mind, what I had retained from all forms of media, including schooling. I had light understanding of an expansive variety of things trivial as well as applicable in daily life, from writing to science, mathematics, art, humor, and the varying cultures of the world, all lacking in specific detail. The framework of storytelling was hardwired as part of my conscious, so I became a mover to pursue that to its extent. My concepts of complex social situations and personal interaction was nonexistent, connected to a predisposition of what felt right at the time. Nuance and minutia I could not understand, yet in moments of rarity had once flowed freely by way of taking instinctive action through the highs of pheromone and chemical balance. I understood without thought. I was sure this led to a segregated, stunted mindset, absent of the perspectives of my fellow man while simultaneously drowning in them.. My mind consistently explored what it did not have or didn't understand.

"What the fuck are you talking about?" Ghostie said through laughter. I had been thinking unaware of her observation.

"Stay in the present for me," she said.

"I'm working on it," I said as my thoughts dissolved.

We viewed a variety of movies of random genres. "Good move," Ghostie would say as the characters were in the middle of action. I watched in silence and slipped into sleep as the night prevailed.

I found myself back in the work room with the Outleyer centered in it, there was no great battle taking place and the creature seemed tame. Its physical form was one of better days, without the yellowing of jaundice and the reddening of broken blood vessels.

"Why here?" I asked once again through our connection. The Outleyer spoke through me.

"To survive
Someway
To stay alive
Someway."

Though I was asking why it was back in the room with me, I began to understand. The entity's connection to me was alive and well by way of my Veil-stained memory, even through the death of its digital body.

I awoke and instantly lost track of the dream and what was said, though I felt it could have been important. I checked where Ghostie was and found her once again staring out into the world from the window. We exchanged a couple of 'mornings'. Shortly after I was dressed there was a knock on the door. The suited woman had arrived. I picked up the heavy papers from the nightstand and handed them to her.

She flipped through them for a long moment, making sure the bulk of the work was done before smiling and saying, "Follow me."

I gathered The Veil device and stuffed it in my front pocket. The three of us exited the room and made our way to the elevator lobby. We took the long trip down looking to exchange buildings and made our way out to the courtyard once again. I struggled to recollect what the buildings comprising the citadel were for. We passed several suits, lab coats and movers as we strolled. We walked for a few minutes to a two-story building, which felt insignificant compared to those surrounding.

"Here, you will be evaluated," the suited woman said and led us inside.

There were rows of transparent glass screens with people behind monitoring them. It was inertly quiet. A bunch of lab coats and faces attached to them surrounded Ghostie and I, breaking the silence. They began congratulating us on the job's completion. I avoided eye contact. They seemed too eager to get to work on us.

One of the men reached out with a plastic container, asking me to, "Please place The Veil device in the bin."

I felt crowded and said, "No," plainly.

As the man was about to press the issue, the suited woman cut him off saying,

"I don't think that will be necessary."

The suited woman then led us to a locker room, giving me a key and a number to one of the lockers and said, "Inside you will find a change of clothes."

I went into the room in which I found several movers, both male and female changing clothes. They all stopped to stare at Ghostie and I. Mostly Ghostie. I noted that none of the other movers had Veiled companions anchored to them. I adverted my eyes as best I could as the bodies of half-naked women that were adorning my vision began causing sensory overload. It had been years since I had seen such sights. Ghostie held back her laughter. I knew she knew what was on my mind. My face went red as I quietly made my way to the assigned locker hidden in the back of the large room. I felt semi-secluded between the rows of lockers and changed as fast as I could into the black sweats and white T-shirt provided. I quickly exited and reunited with the suited woman.

"Everything okay?" the woman asked.

"That was like watching an erotic car accident," Ghostie responded with a quickness.

"Put me back in the fucking crucible already," I replied.

We made our way to a well-lit lab upstairs which included a large metal cylinder with a round glass door beside multiple monitoring devices, a padded chair with a steel table beside it and brightly lit lights above it, a large deep sink, and multiple cabinets which I assumed were filled with tools to cause me pain. The room was cold and felt sterile. A group of lab coats entered after us and introduced themselves, a dentist, a doctor, and a technician. We all shook hands; each hand was colder than the last. We started with the dental work. The dentist moved me to sit down in the padded chair.

I reached out with my mind to Ghostie and told her, "Don't let him microchip me." With a small measure of sarcasm.

He used a cold and wet cloth on my arm, explaining that it was to gather skin cells for veil synchronization. Ghostie and the suited woman watched intently. I pushed my mind to a far-off place as he probed and picked at my teeth which we both thought were in surprisingly decent shape given the circumstances. He then rolled a small machine to my side. I was surprised to see Veiled energy be produced, work its way into my mouth, and mold to it, stopping just short of my throat. It was invasive and numbing but I still preferred it over the sharp utensils that had just been scraping at my gums. He finished quickly, and The Veil retreated into the mechanism.

We then moved to the large saltshaker looking machine where the doctor motioned me to step in. The technician at the monitor turned to give him an 'all clear' and the glass door whirred open. I stepped into the machine and The Veil descended on me, it felt altered, lighter, and it was much less agitating to the skin than I had remembered. The doctor's eyes were on the monitor, along with the technician's. I felt The Veil's mist easily permeate through me in waves of growing intensity. I was not in there for more than a few minutes. Then The Veil had left, gone back up into the machine's lid and the door hummed open. I exited, impressed of how painless physical examination processes had become.

The trio seemed satisfied with the results and left the room.

"So, what was all that about? I thought physical tests were only done prior to workload ins?" I asked the suited woman.

"We have found your brain developed irregularities during your extended time in the Veil. Nothing harmful, just heightened activity in certain areas during time spent communicating with Ghostie, requests, and especially your time connected to the Outleyer," she responded.

"Why does that matter?" I asked. The Company had never seemed so attentive of my health until now.

"Because nobody else here has a partner like me?" Ghostie asked.

"Very good, Ghostie. We have hopes of changing that," the suited woman said.

"You know how she was created? Right?" I asked slightly on edge.

"We have an idea of how it was done, we'll need your help on replicating the process." My mind stretched out in fear of what was implied. The suited woman told us that examinations were completed and after I was done changing into my original clothing had us follow her back to the hotellike room high in the previous building.

"We will soon start building processes for sustaining the consciousness of the deceased within the Veil," said the suited woman.

"When?" I asked.

"Whenever you are ready," she replied.

With that the suited woman left us.

"What do you think, Ghostie? Sounds like people are going to be dying out here," I said, as I paced throughout our room with a racing heart and mind.

"It's probably not what you think it is," she replied calmly. My mind brought up situations of murder, forced by my hand at worst and euthanasia at best.

"I can feel that you're taking this all out of context," Ghostie said. My mind refused to stop believing I would become a killer if I decided to contact the suited woman again. "You should have just asked her what she meant when you spoke with her. Give her a call and I'm sure she could clear everything up," Ghostie said.

"Fuck all that, she's in on it," I said out of paranoia. My mind began the construction of a story in which conspiracies plagued the citadel and the people in it, movers being murdered to push the technology further while The Company capitalized on it.

"I think you've seen too many movies," Ghostie said, aware of my every thought. I sat on the bed to calm down and tried to rationalize what was said by the suited woman, though in my mind it became unclear, the words mixed and twisted while clouded by the rush of possible negative outcomes that we were destined to carry out.

It was late and sleep was elusive. Ghostie rested on her bed and The Veil device was propped up on the nightstand. The floor creaked loudly outside. I sat up from the bed. I could feel movement in the hall. A note slid into my room. I quickly rose to my feet and made my way to the locked door; the pace of footsteps grew as their sound faded. I unlocked and quickly opened the door, looking both ways down the hall. No one was there. I shut and locked the door as quietly as I could and turned my attention to the note. I picked it up and turned it over. It read,

'Meet me in the basement before morning'. With a small map that had one of the outer buildings within the gated compound circled. I woke Ghostie from her resting state and presented the card to her.

"Well, we better get going if we plan to meet them tonight," she said, grabbing The Veil device and placing it on the bed. She began to punch buttons.

"What are you doing?" I asked.

"You'll be a lot less recognizable without me at your side." I watched as her form was transferred into Veiled energy and vacuumed quietly back into the apparatus. I pocketed the device and put on my shoes as the feeling that this was a bad idea filled me.

I felt alone and almost naked without Ghostie beside me as I made my way to the lobby of the hotellike building and exited into the courtyard. Some lingering movers along with a couple suits were still active. I doubted I would be of any particular interest. I referenced the map on the card and started heading in that direction. When I arrived, I looked at the small building, a bit run down and empty looking, abandoned. I entered through automatic doors which I was surprised still functioned, the air was cold and smelled stale. Dim bluish lights flickered throughout the building a couple times before shutting off. I pulled The Veil device out and pushed the buttons, energy seeped from the machine and Ghostie was with me once more. Ghostie focused her eyes to light our path as we made our way to the elevator and pressed the down button, which did not light up. After a moment of waiting, we decide to pursue other options.

"We gotta find a stairwell," Ghostie said.

We did a quick walk around the floor and came across the stairwell door. We went down the flights, four floors deep until the stairs ended and we came across a security door which looked new in comparison to the rest of the building. A face flashed before us in the wired window, and the door opened. A man in technician's attire stood before us. He wore a belt of packed pouches around his waist, full of what I assumed would be wire and tools.

"Mover. Come with me."

"Here we should be free from The Company's eyes," the technician said as we followed him into the room.

"You the one with the notes?" I asked. Figments filled the darkness in my view until the lights came on. Ghostie adjusted her vision accordingly. The room was filled with cables attached to large, defunct, and outdated veil machines and monitors.

"Yes, word reached me that you built a connection to this one years ago," he said motioning to Ghostie as we walked through the room into another stairwell.

"I had hopes of postponing your work until the Outleyer was removed, and the reactor upgraded. They allowed you to proceed despite my protests. I was then informed you had destroyed the beyond-digital anomaly in impressive fashion," he added.

"What are we doing here?" I asked.

"The Company wants you, mover, to cultivate and communicate with the consciousness of those that experience death within The Veil," he replied.

"In order to anchor them to active movers?" Ghostie asked.

"That's only the first part of their plan." We made our way downstairs, dozens of floors underground. I prepared my mind expecting to find jars full of failed human experiments, or to walk in on an alien autopsy. The modern metal architecture shifted to that of stone and steel yellowed and rusted. My body turned heavy as we came upon a hallway lit with old fixtures, and filled with bars of iron, well-worn mortar and stone that traveled far beyond Ghostie's illuminating vision. There were constant changes in air pressure like the atmosphere couldn't make up its mind. I popped my ears continuously trying to find equilibrium.

"What's down here?" I asked as we continued down the hall; the words the technician spoke hit me audibly only after his lips stopped moving.

"Distortion." Thoughts of demise and bodily torture overtook me. Whispers were heard.

"Do not fear pain or death of the physical body."

"What are you?" I asked the captivating voice as the technician and I crumpled under the immense weight of our limbs, the words I spoke reached me as an echo long before I heard them come out of my mouth. I still I felt the need to drive forward.

"Captured. Distorted. Existing."

Ghostie picked us up by our collars in a display of strength and speed. She dragged us sideways into one of the barred and barren rooms lining the hallway, my body still felt heavy. I watched as what looked like the twisting air of heat mirages were breathed in and out, making a humming noise against the iron and stone. The air moved in waves, patterning itself up and down the hallway.

"How much farther do we need to go?" I asked the technician, now free from the echo.

"About half a mile. We'll have only a few minutes after the changing," said the technician.

"What changing?" I asked.

"We should get the fuck out of here," Ghostie said with worry that was well within reason, though she was unaffected by the heaviness taking hold of us. I poked my head outside to be hit by the substantial currents once again. The energy was strange. I wanted to leave.

"You would return."

"Mover. We must not stop here," said the technician as he left the momentary relief of the walled off room.

I attempted to grab him and pull him back to safety, but as I reached for him, I found myself motivated to follow. We climbed forward until I felt something familiar, a separation of physical touch from physique, like the second skin of The Veil leaving me. I pushed past it now feeling lighter than ever and turned to watch both my body and that of the technician collapse and lay dormant before me. I looked down at my hands, my legs, the appearance, and clothing were unchanged, it was my body, just free from the weight of muscle and bone, free from the limiting air that had been burning my lungs. Before turning forwards again I observed Ghostie following closely. Our movement down the hall became unnaturally nimble. The three of us burst down the corridor, and something was near, something strange and strong. There was a figure in the distance. We fought against the airwaves which pushed and pulled like the hallway itself was breathing. I stayed mindful of Ghostie's distance from The Veil device.

"She cannot be bound by such a machine. Not here."

We approached the faceless figure swathed in energy and the three of us poised ourselves against its breath. It casted deep colors and shapes that churned in stark contrast to the dark air around it. I felt odd as we closed in. I tried to keep track of time spent away from our bodies.

"Back to the shells in time, I have been here mere decades. Pacing."

"What is The Company planning?" I asked despite my hesitation.

"To continue harvesting, without the burdens of flesh."

"So, it's true? What can we do to stop this?" Ghostie asked.

"Should you do something to stop this? That would lessen the oncoming struggle of many, though my existence would be questionable."

"Are you the source of The Veil's technology?" I asked.

"The machines are of feeble mimicry. I am not connected to them directly, though potentially the anomalies."

"What should we do?" I asked.

"Whatever you must. This may prove useful." The faceless figure extended its arm and opened its hand revealing a small box, of black, untextured material. The being gestured for me to take it. I reached my hand out to grab it through the swirls of strange matter. I opened the container and found another Veil device, small yet more advanced in appearance, with a single button raised amongst that same untextured material. I gave the empty box back to the figure.

"What is this?"

"A boon of sorts. Forged in a crucible of my own making, it is bound to what was once felt, and affixed to you specifically. In return, I require something to be returned."

The figure connected to me, cleaner than anything I've yet to experience with The Veil thus far. He searched my thoughts, pulling every memory tarnished by the Outleyer to the foreground, and took them into him.

"We have had our time. Back to the shells. Now."

"Did you kill Ghostie?" I asked. The wind picked up.

"Did you kill Ghostie?" I asked again with emphasis.

I resisted against the gusts hoping for more answers. The figure's breath drew us in for a moment and its force was multiplied as it exhaled, steadily pushing us back towards our dormant bodies. The wind in the tunneled hallway faltered as we found ourselves. My sense of touch split between my veiled form and my physical double as I closed in. I placed The Veil machine in my copy's hands, closed my eyes, and returned to myself. Breath entered my lungs along with the now lofty weight of my body, encased in a numbness which I strained to move my muscles against. I pocketed the small device, checked, ensuring Ghostie was with me and glanced at the technician who looked to be fighting a similar numbness. We helped each other to our feet and quickly but clumsily made our way to the stairwell with pins and needles electrifying my entire body. We mobbed halfway up the unending stairwell before pausing for breath. We realized we were not in immediate danger when we finished the long trek back to the room that housed the outdated Veil technology.

"Have you met that thing before?" I asked the technician as we both collapsed at the top of the stairs. I was fighting for air yet again.

"Once before, long ago. Told me to keep an eye on you," he said seriously.

"What can we do to stop The Company?" Ghostie asked.

"There is no stopping The Company. Their reach is too great and their people too many, but this compound is the sole location of veiled technology development," he said.

"So, we shut down the digital reactors?" I asked.

"Disabling their source of veiled energy transfer would be paramount in slowing their work down, and much easier than destroying each reactor individually. I'm working on something that can disable it without putting movers in The Veil at risk. You two should go back to your room, we will talk more later."

I pressed buttons on Ghostie's veil device, and she was transferred into energy that receded back into the contraption. I then walked, as nonchalantly as I could, out of the building. It was dark outside and there were no remaining suits or movers wandering the courtyard, security was stationed at the base of the hotellike building. I passed them without any questioning. I made my way back to our hotellike room and set both veil devices on Ghostie's bed. I tapped at buttons until Ghostie was with me again.

"What do you think it does?" Ghostie asked as we stared at the newly acquired technology.

"The figure said it could help us. That it was bound to what was once felt," I said.

"Well, only one way to find out," Ghostie said as she pressed the lone button.

I was expecting The Veil's recognizable staticky shimmer, what came forth were whisps of unclosed circles and crescents that wrapped around and radiated from the machine, the shapes sought me out and pervaded my skin.

"Oh fuck!" I said and lurched over.

"What is it?" Ghostie asked.

My soul was not flayed from my body as I had expected, and I did not gain any noticeable strength in mind or body. I felt no change nor feeling from the device. I was slightly disappointed.

"I don't feel anything," I said through laughter.

"You dirty fucker," Ghostie said as she shoved me into the room's wall. "Whoops," She said.

"Hold on. Shove me again," I said, Ghostie pushed me with force once more.

"Slap me," I said.

"If you say so," she said as she cocked her arm back and hit me across the face with a resounding snap.

I couldn't feel it, the contact of her hand, my body as it connected with the wall. I took a moment to think.

"Strength," I said in hopes of changing the device's effect on me. I felt my heartbeat through my eardrums as blood pumped into my muscles. I searched the room for something to test myself with. I grabbed the deck of cards we had used to play games with and pressed my thumb into them. I pushed with everything I had, and they began to separate and break apart until my fingers met each other.

"Back to normal," I said. The supreme power that had come so abruptly left me, bruises formed on my fingertips and the sting from Ghostie's hand began to spread across my face. My curiosity of the device was growing, and the possibilities of its application were multiplying. I pondered the opportunities of such a clean connection to advanced crucible energy.

"Maybe we should save this for the right time," she said and pressed the button once more.

The crescents fled from me and made their way back into the device. It was late in the night, and we decided we had better get some sleep before daybreak. I lay on the bed still in my jeans and hooded sweatshirt, thinking about how strange the events in the past few months had been. Ghostie played an action romance movie and soon I gave into my dreams.

I retraced my time in the room. Ghostie was once again tickling my peripheral vision, and a choice lay before me. To let her suffer the rest of my days as a phantom, anomalous in her own right, or to destroy The Veiled device in which she was bound to. To release her and let her experience death a second time. To go through whatever it was that the spirit of humankind naturally undergoes when it is released from the shell of physical existence. To move on. Though I realized it had always been a decision, there was still no choice I could make. Thoughts formed.

"Stay with me, at least for now, ghost. Let's use what time we have, together."

I woke up late in the morning, she was staring out the window again. "Ghostie," I said.

"What's up?" she said.

I thought of everything I wanted to say and ask her. Nerves hit me.

"Let's go out on that date," I said.

I cleaned up, showering, shaving my near grungy beard clean, and I grabbed some fresh clothes out of the drawers. A button-up shirt and some slacks were the most formal clothes I could find. A bit of a mismatch with the new tennis shoes.

"Are you sure this is the right time for this?" Ghostie asked.

"No, come on, let's go," I said.

I stashed both Veil devices in my pockets. We made our way to the cafeteria on the second floor where breakfast was being served. It felt good to get out of the room again. We weren't alone. A couple groups of movers and suits were sitting at the tables sending us long stares as if someone were taking a ghost to breakfast. I grabbed some free coffee and poured five packs of sugar into it. I decided to skip the food out of respect, and we made our way to a booth. We sat down and I got straight into it.

"So, what do you think, Ghostie, would you have been happier if you hadn't been affixed to The Veil, to me?" I asked.

"I'm not sure, when we first found each other, I felt like nothing, energy locked in a mix of more energy. We had to get our communication and language down, which was a huge learning experience, and then, well... we've always had a job to do. Everyone had a job to do. The question of dying never really came to me. I guess I was too busy trying to stay alive in whatever shape I could. With the new Veil device, it's like I'm almost human again, I mean I know I might not look it, but it really does feel close," she said.

"That's good to hear," I said, relieved. "I want to try something with the new device. Suit or mover?" I asked quietly and pressed the button on the gift from the faceless figure. Ghostie stole a glance at the still wide-eyed tables.

"Suit for sure."

I reached out in a one-way connection, locating his mind and tying it off with intent of sending something, it was so damn smooth with the new device. I ran through my mind for crucible tests over the years until I settled on something recent and fitting while still humane enough to try on one of the suits who couldn't look away from her.

"Tears of joy."

I finished drinking my coffee while watching the build up until the man burst into heavy sobs and scrambled to wipe at the tears running down his face. This tore the attention off Ghostie. I got up and placed my empty mug into the dish bin. Before we left, I gave the guy a pat on the back and reassured him.

"I felt the same way when I first met her, man."

We made our way back to the elevator lobby and the doors opened.

"Back to normal," I said and severed the connection to my victim. We found our way to the room again. My mind was still on the application of experiences in the emotional crucible. One specifically. One that was discontinued early on. One of pain.

We entered our room, and the phone was ringing. It was the suited woman, and she was displeased with our unprofessional conduct just moments earlier. Word travelled quickly; everyone knew of us by way of Ghostie. She wanted to know if we were ready for process creation.

I insisted on a few more free days, stalling with hope the technician would contact us in that time.

"Fine. I can allow two more days, but after that we must move forward," she said.

Feeling a bit restricted in the formal wear, I took my original clothes into the bathroom and changed into the familiar attire. We were back to playing the waiting game. Though I woke up late, the day was dragging. We passed on the various electronic experiences in favor of video games to kill time. We watched in glee as Ghostie's character ripped the head off my character's body in a bloody spectacle.

"Yes! That was awesome!" she exclaimed.

"That's five-five. Wanna go for a tiebreaker?" I asked.

"Let's save it for tomorrow," she said. I turned the TV off and laid down. I heard a note slide under my door. I picked it up and it read in the same handwriting,

'The Company is on to me, basement tomorrow night'.

I showed it to Ghostie.

"Fuck, if they're on to him they might be on to us," she said.

"We don't know that for sure," I said.

The next day was longer than the last. We didn't want to play games or watch television.

"You know we don't have to shut the power down. We could leave now and be done with all this. They won't have any immediate replacements for us."

"They would eventually, and even if we shut down this operation, I'm sure more will follow. Let's go for a walk," I told Ghostie.

"Where are we going now?" she asked.

"To the bar."

"You're going drinking?"

"Not exactly… Well, maybe one or two." We walked out of our current building and made our way to the tower that held our original workroom along with the bar.

"Mover! What can I get you?" he asked.

"Something sugary please, and do you have anything for Ghostie?" I responded. I watched as he quickly whipped up a beverage consisting of ice-cold chocolate liqueurs and creams.

"Here we are. And for you Ghostie…" he started.

The barman pulled a large box shaped machine that began to whirr as he started it.

"…Something for feeling rather than taste I'm afraid."

"Um I think I'll be okay."

"Nonsense. Place your hands here." He said as he finished its calibration.

The heat of the machine was melting the ice in my drink. I watched closely as Ghostie put her hands on the contraption. I could hear a buzz and see pops of electricity form around her fingertips.

"Whoa," she said as the motor of the machine seemed to die.

"How do you feel?" the barman asked.

"Overcharged," she said sounding slightly loopy.

I turned my attention back to the reason we came here.

"Barman, I've come to ask if you have any more of those stimulants."

"I do indeed. Though are you sure you'll find them necessary in your off time?"

"Let's call it a precaution."

"I see," he said and crouched behind the bar for a moment before setting two of the bottles on the table.

"What do we owe you?" I asked as I stood up and pocketed the stimulants.

"Not a thing," the barman replied.

We went back to our room in the hotellike building. Nightfall was approaching. I made preparations in the likely case that we couldn't make it back to the room. I called room service and asked for a backpack to be delivered. It arrived promptly. I put the faceless figure's gift into the tip of my shoe, where I could activate it by applying pressure with my big toe. I wrapped up the charger and wires to Ghostie's Veil device and stuffed them into the backpack. It would be a shame if the two devices fell into The Company's hands.

"You ready?" I asked.

"As I'll ever be," she said. I pressed the buttons on her machine, and she dissipated before me. I stuck one of the two stimulant bottles in the pack and zipped it up. I made it to the elevator lobby where I downed an entire bottle of stimulants, choking on the burning feeling without the power of The Veil aiding. I kept them down. I headed outside and started the trek to the run-down building where we had first met the technician. The night was dark but with stimulants in me everything seemed brighter, more alive. There were a few guards posted outside the various buildings, I ignored the lingering suits and movers that remained outside. I was relieved to see nobody positioned in front of the deteriorating structure. I entered and pulled Ghostie's device from the backpack. I punched the buttons until she was free to walk with me once again. We found the stairwell and walked the stairs until we came to the security door. The technician's face flashed in the window, and he opened the door. He wasn't alone. The suited woman was there, along with six guards armed with batons that began to surround us. I figured Ghostie and I could take them.

"Let's ice these fuckers and get outta here," she said silently through our connection.

"Hold on for me," I replied. The suited woman looked displeased with the three of us and started talking. I ignored her and hit the button to the figure's gift in my shoe and started a two-way connection with the technician.

"What's the play here, man?" I asked, doing my best to avoid turning my head to him.

"I have a disruptor necessary for destroying the power supply."

"Do you know where the supply is located?"

"Yes. When they move us to their garrison, we will have our chance."

"Shouldn't we try to take them out here?"

"No, we will need them to get passed the security doors."

"Gotcha," I said and severed the connection. The suited woman went through the backpack, found Ghostie's device, and shut it down. As she disappeared, one of the guards delivered a crushing blow to my ribcage that could be felt even through the painkilling effect of the stimulants.

"Sorry I wasn't paying attention," I said as I gathered myself.

"Why are you here?" said the suited woman.

"This isn't where they host bingo night?" I asked.

Another blow was delt, this time to my back.

"Take them to be processed, our plans will continue with or without them," she said. The guards took us to their tower of modern architecture, I took great care to keep my foot off The Veil device as we walked through the lobby. We exited the elevators and passed through multiple security doors, opened by retinal scanners and handprints that the guards had clearance with. I watched as one of the guards took my backpack to a sealed room. I pressed down on the device in my shoe and formed a one-way connection to the man as he escaped my vision. The technician and I were locked in a room together far down the hall. I took the active veil device out of my shoe and pocketed it. We sat in the room and planned our next move.

"Where are we headed from here?" I asked.

"We need to go seven floors up where the Veiled energy is distributed to their reactors for programming. Once we're there one of us will have to use this on the charging tank that converts electricity into veiled energy," he said, pulling a disc the size of a large coin from his pocket.

"That thing is gonna destroy The Veil?" I asked.

"Not exactly, but it will function as a puncture in the tank, funneling the raw veiled energy out from the reactors, disrupting the constant flow and breaking the circuit essentially. Unpinned to a specific point, the funneled energy will be uncharged and unstable," said the technician.

"What does that mean, is it going to explode?" I asked.

"No, but if we are in the room when the device goes off, there will be consequences."

"Okay. Are you ready to move, technician?" I asked.

"I think I'm ready."

"I estimate this room is within Ghostie's range."

It was unfortunate that none of the guards decided to stay with us.

"I have a connection with one of the guards in the room with her," I said.

I was hoping to spare at least some of their lives.

"Better use it then, I don't see us getting out of here anytime soon."

I paused.

"There's gotta be some other way man," I said.

"Just do it, mover! We have no chance to stop them in here!" I reluctantly began probing the security guard's mind, it was difficult at this range, even with the new device. I watched what he was doing through his eyes and unloaded deep panic and fear into him. I did my best to copy the Outleyer's technique. I lied to him using his own voice, creepy as I could muster.

"Open the backpack and you will be spared." With crucible fear in him he obliged.

"Take The Veil device," I coerced him by moving my hands in tandem with his.

"These buttons in this order," we said. I began to guide his hands through the process of releasing Ghostie. The device clicked on, and the room turned red right before I could sever the connection. I heard a door open, and slam shut far down the hall. Then screams. The cracking of bones. More screams. The heavy slap of torn flesh against the wall. More screams. With the sounds being made outside I was glad to be behind a locked door.

"The fuck is going on out there!" the technician asked with concern.

"Wait for it," I said. Blood trickled into the locked room from the space beneath the door, followed by silence. The screams in the hall outside died down and the door to our cell sprang open, Ghostie had one of the guard's arms in one hand and half of a head, severed at the jaw, grasped by its hair, in the other. Both were leaking blood onto the already drenched floor.

"The doors are open," she said as her image flickered with drops of red fluid not knowing whether to fall from or stick to her digital body.

"That's my girl," I said. I walked to where the backpack was being held, careful to not slip on the numerous crimson pools that soaked the ground. I downed my last bottle of stimulants and heard the technician behind me yell.

"Jesus Christ, mover!" he exclaimed, slipping on the bloody ground.

"Fuck man, I told you. Ghostie, don't kill anyone else," I replied. We hurried up the stairs, guards flooded after us from floors below. The figure's gift was in my hands. I activated it, instantly connecting to the guard in front, telling him to take a break. I heard him scream in pain but didn't stop to watch his legs give out from beneath him. He fell and stalled the guards behind him. We were halfway to our floor when security started piling in from above us. Ghostie was occupied with bending one of the guard's fingers too far in the wrong direction, I stole a baton from him and whispered.

"Strength." I aimed for hands and eyes hoping they would not be able to fight without them as we continued the slow crawl upstairs, it was becoming increasingly warm in the cold stairwell. I was hit repeatedly. The slick, stinging of salty sweat mixed with blood in the cuts before it fell from me. I passed the baton to the technician who was holding the high ground from the usurpers below. Ghostie blinded those above with her vision and I began targeting joints. Stimulants in me, and the strength of the figure's boon, my enemies felt slow, and the separation of bone and tendon was effortless. I was unfettered by the sudden protrusion of skeletal structure and strange presentation of anatomy ripped from the delicate protection of tissue and skin. We stepped past the pile of still breathing bodies, and the ones still on their feet farther below us hesitated, questioning their approach. We worked to our door, and the technician locked it behind us.

"Back to normal," I said searching for air. The strength left me with a lingering soreness prevailing.

"Where is it?" I asked the technician.

"Follow me," he said. Ghostie and I chased after him. We came upon a double wide security door; I could see a lightshow of energy transmutation even through the thick protective windows. The technician pried the panel free from the wall underneath the screen signaling for a handprint and began hitting switches and exposing wires.

"How long?" I asked. There was movement down the hall, the suited woman had brought a dozen guards with her from the elevator lobby.

"A minute or two," said the technician who was knee deep in exposed wires and circuit boards.

"We'll hold them," Ghostie said.

"Mover!" said the suited woman. "Stop this right now, you are putting everyone within The Veil's life at risk!"

I turned to the technician who shot a glance at me.

"Wrong," he assured before turning back to the wires.

"What does that matter if you're planning to enslave them after death?" I asked.

"That is not what we are trying to do here."

"Then what is it you are trying to do?"

"Make progress," she said. The woman pulled a veil device similar in craft to Ghostie's from her pocket. She began pressing buttons and Ghostie's form was scattered.

"Ghost?" I asked. No response. I punched buttons on her device and her glitched body was vacuumed back into the safety of her machine. The woman was trying to form some type of one-way connection with me. She said something into the device and a terrible, sharp soreness was felt throughout my body. It was painful to be sure, but wasn't far off from the crucible levels I was once locked in. I pressed on the figure's gift to me and began making connections of my own. I linked all the guards one by one to my own mind. Everyone down the hall was going to feel this.

"Pain!" I exclaimed.

The feeling was sobering, crippling, and sharper than anything within memory. The crucible-like energy within the figure's gift was truly something to behold. The entirety of my body felt as though red-hot knives were sunk into me and twisted continuously. The guards fell to the ground, and through my connection I ensured they felt every bit of what I was experiencing. I fell to my knees. I knew the agony I was encased in would pass quickly if I could manage stay conscious longer than the guards and shut the device down. The woman was still standing, and I could not manage a connection to her.

"That's enough mover!" the suited woman exclaimed.

"How much longer?" I asked the technician.

"A few more moments!" he exclaimed. I pushed past the pain, enduring it with everything I had, forcing my eyes to remain open. The room was starting to spin, but I could feel the guards dropping out of consciousness. I was unable to hold the pain in me any longer.

"Back to normal," I said, and the pain began to fade. Two of the guards who managed to stay awake got up and started after me. I severed my connection to them as they tackled me to the ground.

"Strength," I said. Blood hit my muscles and I now had a chance. I grabbed at one of the hands pinning me down and gripped it with all my power, he screamed and tried to pull away, but I was locked in, I felt the crunch as his bones were powdered between my palm and fingers. He reeled backwards and fell limply against the wall. With one guard down I could focus on the one remaining. I lifted him off me and dove on him, sprawling my legs to keep him on his stomach. I forced a chokehold onto him, careful to apply only enough pressure necessary for him to pass out and not pass away. His body turned into dead weight in my arms.

"Back to normal," I said once more. The security door opened, and the technician helped me to my feet.

"Let's go, mover," he said. We rushed through the door. There were two connected, metal pylons filling the center of the room. The top one spanned several floors above, tapering down in thickness to meet the bottom one with a small, clear box of glass between them where electricity to veil energy transference occurred. The monstrous machines reverbed a humming sound at steady pace and flashes of deep, colorful light radiated from the small box betwixt them.

Déjà vu hit me as technician pulled the coin-like apparatus from his pocket and fixed it to the glass box. The suited woman could be heard down the hall. I could only assume more guards were on their way.

"Mover!" she yelled. With her Veil device she still posed a threat to us. I could not endanger Ghostie if I were to engage her.

"This is where we part ways, mover," said the technician with seriousness.

"All right, tell me how to activate the device," I responded and held my backpack up to his chest, motioning for him to take it.

"Take Ghostie and get as far away from here as possible," I continued. The technician looked stoic.

"That's not part of the plan. You have already been down this road, mover. It's my turn to close the distortion cycle." I did not understand what he meant, but I could read the seriousness in his voice. He pushed the outstretched backpack to my chest and slowly walked me backwards through the doorway.

"See you soon," he said before pressing buttons to the interface on his side. The heavy metal door slammed closed, sealing the entryway between us. The suited woman was now beside me and noticed what was happening. We watched through the safety of the door and the light fog of the thick glass as the man activated the device. The sounds of the machine became louder, and louder as raw veiled energy was diverted from the pylons, spreading into the room before becoming affixed to the technician and encompassing him. Colors swirled around him in patterns as the pylons became noticeably reddened with heat. His body became without form, then, the shape of a man outlined in darkness, projecting energy, twisted and colorful. The faceless figure was standing before me once more. Either my vision of him, or the figure itself began flashing, from being there in this glorious display of patterned radiance to nothing, repeatedly. He let out a half-human scream that shook the floor and flickered the lights before the energy closed around him and he was gone.

I snapped back to the current situation and pushed the suited woman down before making my way through the open security doors to the elevator. I was unsure if she was in shock or trying to make sense of what had just unfolded, for she did not follow me. The ride down must have taken hours. I entered the lobby which was to my surprise, clear. I ran through the door and kept running without looking back. I was able to see gates of the compound. They were large and heavy, speared at the tips of the individual iron bars. I ran towards them and dug Ghostie's device along with the figure's gift from the backpack in hopes of using its power one last time. Ghostie appeared before me, disconnected from the suited woman's hold, and quickly matched my pace.

"The Gate!" I exclaimed. I activated the second device and spoke into the figure's gift. "All of my strength." I squatted down and grabbed the horizontal, bottom bar. Ghostie fell into synch with me, and we lifted hard against the gate. The iron lurched but did not give way.

"On three," she said. Voices of guards could be heard rallying behind us. We did not have time to look back and I was unsure if we could take another encounter with the them.

"One." I could hear rushed footsteps closing in. A frail ghost and my meager flesh were our last chance at freedom.

"Two." The mixture of undiscernible voices and yelling was growing louder. Sweat leaked from me and I felt cold in the night's wind.

"Three." We lifted with every bit of strength we had. The Iron lurched loudly again until the bottom hinge was torn free from its fasteners with a stupendous ring, we then had leverage against the top hinge, and rose from a squatting position to a standing one. The metal groaned before surrendering to our combined strength. The top hinge broke away from the frame. We had an exit, and we took it. Free from the compound, we fled down the sidewalk until the sound of steps behind us were no longer present. We ran until the stimulants wore off and then ran